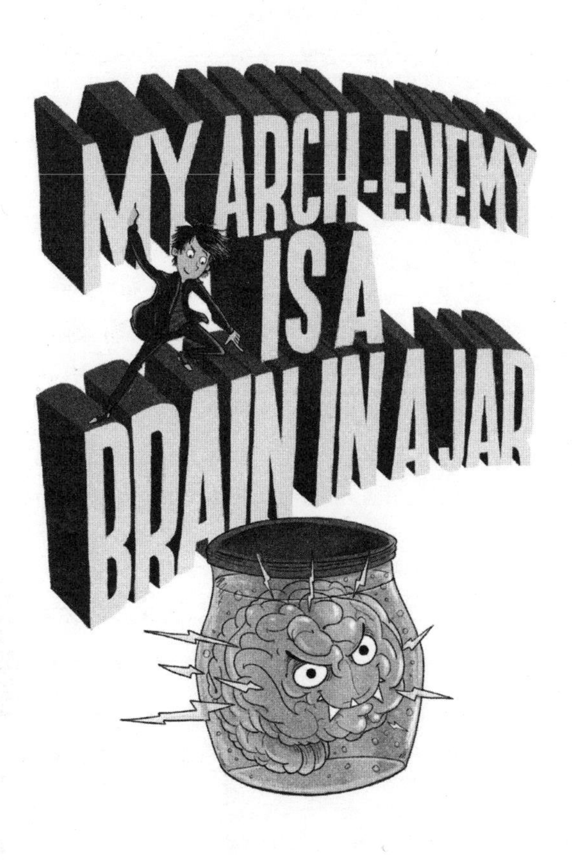
MY ARCH-ENEMY
IS A
BRAIN IN A JAR

OUT OF THIS WORLD REVIEWS FOR
MY BROTHER IS A SUPERHERO

"I even think my dad would like reading this book!"
David, The Book Squad, The Beano

"Cosmic! Amazing! Outstanding! Probably the funniest book I have read for a long time."
Alison A. Maxwell-Cox, The School Librarian

"I was so addicted to it that my mum had to make me put it down."
Calum, aged 11

"Funny, fast moving and deftly plotted, it's the best thing to hit the superhero world since sliced kryptonite."
Damian Kelleher, Dad Info

"You know a book is going to be good when you're giggling after five minutes... Ideal for comic readers and superhero experts."
Nicola Lee, The Independent

"An excellent adventure story with real heart that's also properly funny."
Andrea Reece, Lovereading4Kids

"You'll laugh until you fall out of your tree house!"
Steve Coogan

"A brilliantly funny adventure with twists, turns, crazy characters and a really hilarious ending. Fantastic!"
Sam, aged 11

"Brilliantly funny."
The Bookseller

MY ARCH-ENEMY IS A BRAIN IN A JAR

DAVID SOLOMONS

First published in the UK in 2018 by Nosy Crow Ltd
The Crow's Nest, 14 Baden Place
Crosby Row, London, SE1 1YW, UK

www.nosycrow.com

ISBN: 978 0 85763 991 2

A CIP catalogue record for this book is available from the British Library.

Printed and bound in the UK by Clays Ltd, Elcograf S.p.A.
Typeset by Tiger Media

Papers used by Nosy Crow are made from wood grown in sustainable forests

3 5 7 9 10 8 6 4

For my mum and dad

Are we nearly there yet?

1
LUKE WHO'S TALKING

My brother is a superhero, and *I* am my brother.

Somewhere on the way back from a parallel Earth, Zack and I had swapped bodies. My eleven-year-old mind was in his fourteen-year-old body, and vice versa. I shuddered at the thought. I didn't even like wearing his hand-me-down trousers, so to think that I was in his actual skin? *Yeuch*.

I stared at him – *me* – across the floor of the tree house. I'd never seen myself like this before – mirrors don't tell you the truth, and my Evil Twin had better hair. (Side-note: lots of people have cousins who live in a different part of the country; I have a superpowered twin

in another dimension. Also, a cousin in Birmingham). I looked myself up and down. My Spider-Man T-shirt was as amazing on me as expected, but I didn't appear as tall as I'd hoped and I was definitely on the skinny side. Moreover, at that moment my face was pinched with concern, but I put that down to Zack.

He was frowning at Zorbon the Decider, representative of the High Council of Frodax Wonthreen Rrr'n'fargh, mysterious bestower of superpowers, and the garishly purple-costumed alien who'd landed us in this body-swap horror story. We'd travelled home from another universe together on his interdimensional bus earlier that afternoon. During the course of the journey, Zorbon had shrunk from the height of a basketball player to something approaching R2-D2 proportions. He explained that crossing dimensions could do strange things. No kidding.

As Zack glowered and Zorbon gave his best all-knowing expression, I realised for the first time that the unfortunate situation had thrown up one very interesting consequence. In all the fuss it had almost slipped me by. If I was Zack, then that meant…

"I have superpowers!"

I heard my brother let out a long groan. He could complain all he liked. I had more important matters to attend to: I was desperate to try out my new-found abilities. First I'd go with a bit of telekinesis, then maybe I'd telepathically sneak into Dad's head and discover his secret Christmas-present hiding place, after that definitely some flying—

"They're not yours," Zack snapped. "They're mine."

"You didn't even want them in the first place," I reminded him. "They're in the right hands now. Technically they're still your hands, but I'm in control." I wiggled my fingers to demonstrate.

"Well, we've all seen what happens when *you* get powers."

He was referring to Stellar, my Evil Twin. And yes, it was true that he had made some questionable decisions while using his powers, but that didn't mean I would.

"Just don't muck about with them," Zack added despairingly.

"Should I even pretend I'm going to pay attention to that?"

I had superpowers. Finally! Sure, it wasn't exactly the way I'd hoped. Along with telekinesis, telepathy, flight and the rest, I had gained terrible dress sense and a one-sided longing for my neighbour's big sister. But still, I was in the body of *a superhero*. My greatest dream had become a reality. When Zorbon first visited the tree

house I had missed out on becoming Star Lad and my world was thrown into confusion. Today, the natural order of things had been restored.

I aimed my telekinetic power at a comic lying on the floor of the tree house and concentrated. "Up, up, up," I mumbled. But the comic didn't move. I didn't give it a second thought. A minor teething problem at most.

What I needed was a mission. Something to test my new abilities.

That was Zorbon's department. From what Zack had told me of their meetings, whenever Zorbon visited he always left a hot, spicy clue to what lay in store. Kind of like a trans-dimensional pizza delivery guy. Usually Zorbon hung around just long enough to tease this world-shattering threat before scarpering. But today Zack wasn't giving him a chance to get the slightest mystic prophecy into the conversation.

"Can't you do something?" Zack pleaded, his voice – *my* voice – rising to a squeak of horror. "You must be able to change us back."

"THAT IS BEYOND MY POWER," Zorbon said. "HOWEVER, THE EFFECT IS TEMPORARY. YOU WILL RETURN TO YOUR OWN BODIES. IN TIME."

"But when exactly?" Zack asked.

"HARD TO SAY," said Zorbon.

"Try," Zack insisted.

Maybe *this* was the mission. Body swaps happened a lot in comics. There were rules. "Presumably there's some sort of fabled object we can go on a quest for that will reverse the effect. Y'know, a mysterious old lamp, an ancient stone, a fuzzy sweater?" The other two looked at me. "A *magically imbued* fuzzy sweater, of course."

Zorbon shook his head gravely. Well, that was a poor show – what kind of curse didn't have a fabled object to undo its effects? But just when it seemed as if the outlook was all doom and gloom, Zorbon raised one thin eyebrow.

"SOME SAY A REVERSE MAY BE TRIGGERED THROUGH STILLNESS AND SILENCE."

Zack tutted at me in disgust. "No chance then. You can't sit still for two minutes and you can't keep your mouth shut for two seconds."

Hanging out with my Evil Twin I'd got used to being insulted by myself, so I didn't rise to the bait. It was clear that, for now at least, we were stuck this way. I looked out across the garden towards the house, where Mum and Dad were busy inside. I may have been craving an implacable foe, but there were already two in the kitchen. ("Implacable" means cold-hearted and ruthless, and is

not, as my friend Lara believes, a word to describe teeth resistant to cavities.)

"What are we going to tell *them*?" I muttered.

The last time they'd seen either of us was during a rampage by a world-eating monster in the town centre at the weekend. I'd had to give them the slip, ducking out of a rescue helicopter during the emergency evacuation. By my reckoning that had been two days ago.

I felt Zack at my side. "They must be going out of their minds with worry."

This would be the second time we'd returned home following a cataclysmic event, armed with a flimsy explanation for our absence. Once our parents got over their relief that we hadn't been squished beneath a giant interdimensional sandal, they were bound to grow suspicious. And there's only so many times you can play the I-got-bumped-on-the-head-and-suffered-temporary-amnesia card.

"THEY ARE NOT CONCERNED ABOUT YOU. AT LEAST, NO MORE THAN USUAL."

"How do you know that?" asked Zack.

I narrowed my eyes in suspicion at Zorbon. "Yeah, what have you done?"

"I MERELY SUBSTITUTED THEIR—"

"Minds? Memories?"

"TEABAGS."

"Come again?"

"IN YOUR LANGUAGE IT IS CALLED *THE INFUSION OF OBLIVION*. THEY WILL REMEMBER THE EVENTS OF THE LAST FEW DAYS BUT NOT YOUR ROLE IN THEM."

"You drugged them?" Zack was outraged.

I was not so offended. A drink that made your parents forget what you'd done? *Yowzah!* "Got any spare?"

"THERE IS ONE MORE THING." Zorbon pulled himself to his full height, which currently lay somewhere around my belly button. "IT IS VITAL THAT YOU PAY HEED TO MY NEXT WORDS."

The air crackled with anticipation. Here it came – Zorbon the Decider's Big Mystic Message. Would his latest forecast be up there with "Nemesis is coming"? We were about to find out.

"DO NOT LET THEM OPERATE HEAVY MACHINERY FOR TWENTY-FOUR HOURS."

As far as uncanny prophecies went that was something of a let-down.

"Is that it?" I asked, not trying to conceal my disappointment. "What about the giant space lizards?"

Zorbon's bald head creased with puzzlement. "I DID NOT MENTION ANY GIANT SPACE LIZARDS."

"Exactly," I said. "Where's my Evil Horde? Army of the Undead? Come on, I've got superpowers now – I need a supervillain to battle."

"Well, I don't," Zack sighed. "All I seem to do lately is avert one apocalypse after another. Honestly, I'd love a break from saving the world."

I started to complain but it was no use. Zorbon wouldn't be dropping another hair-raising adventure in our laps this time. After clarifying that he would also not be dishing out free samples of the Infusion of Oblivion, he announced his departure. He had to be on the other side of the universe by supper-time. With a swish of his purple cape he swept out. He may not have been leaving us with a mission but he could answer one thing for me.

"Keeping busy then?" I asked him.

Zorbon paused, one foot already out of the door. "YES."

"Lot of Deciding to do, I imagine."

"LOTS." He turned to me. "I FEEL THE WEIGHT OF YOUR UNASKED QUESTION, LIKE A REFRIGERATOR IN THE WIND."

He was right. Weird, but right. I'd been burning to ask him this particular question since we were introduced on board the 227 bus on the way back from my Evil Twin's world. I didn't waste any more time. "Here's the thing.

Zack was a mistake, right?"

"Hey!" my brother objected.

"What I mean is, when you showed up here that first time to give out superpowers, you meant to choose me. Didn't you?"

Zorbon's frame filled the lower half of the doorway. A gust of wind caught his tea-towel-sized cape and it flapped around his shoulders. He gazed up at me, the stars on his chest pulsing. "ONE DAY, LUKE PARKER, YOU WILL COME TO UNDERSTAND." Without uttering another word he turned on his tiny heel and left.

Un-ac-cept-able. That was no kind of answer. Unless... "So that's what this whole Freaky Friday thing is about?" I shouted after him, shaking my fist at his departing figure. "Well, if you think by swapping lives with my brother I am going to experience a deeper and more sympathetic understanding of him, then forget it. I refuse."

But Zorbon had gone. He melted into the xenon mist from whence he came. (You just disappear into regular mist, but when it comes to notable varieties of mist – like xenon, or eldritch – you can only return *from whence*).

"This is disastrous," said Zack. He paced around the tree house and wailed. "I have exams in less than three months – if you're still in my body, I'll fail. Everything.

You're going to ruin my life."

My brain-box brother had just sat several mock GCSEs a year early – the real ones were up next. I ignored him and strolled out of the tree house.

"This reminds me of that time I borrowed Dad's car," I said, climbing down the rope ladder, which was a lot easier in Zack's body than it ever had been in my own.

"If I recall correctly," said Zack, stumbling down behind me, "you managed to reverse halfway along the driveway before veering into a hedge."

I waited for him on the ground, grinning at the memory. "Pretty impressive bit of driving, for an eight-year-old. One point three litres of diesel power – all mine to wield. And now this." I gestured up and down my temporary body.

Zack frowned. "Are you comparing me to a Fiat Punto?"

He missed his footing on the next rung, let out a cry and fell the last metre, landing with a thud. He grumbled as I helped him to his feet. "How do you manage to get through a day in this body?"

We crossed the garden and went into the house. Mum and Dad sat at the kitchen table, deep in discussion. Next to two empty cups of tea, a glossy brochure lay open before them.

"This is great. I never win anything," said Dad.

"Uh, don't forget you won my hand in marriage," said Mum.

"Yeah, that was a very odd scratch card."

Mum gave a cry of mock outrage and then Dad held her hand and I could tell that they were about to smooch. I coughed loudly. Mum turned at the interruption, peering at us with laser-sharp interest. "You two seem … different. What's going on?"

For a second I was sure that Zorbon's fancy tea hadn't worked.

"We've swapped bodies," announced Zack.

I had to give him credit – it was an excellent response. Mum and Dad would never believe something that unlikely.

Dad sat up. "Like when Superman swapped bodies with Batman? Or when Superman swapped with the Flash, or Superman and Jimmy Olsen, or Superman and—"

He reeled off several more examples. This body-swap thing really did happen a lot to Superman.

Mum rolled her eyes. "Why do I even ask?" She drew our attention to the brochure on the table. "You're just in time to hear the good news – we're going on holiday."

"After everything that's happened," said Dad, "it'll

be good to get away for a few days. Let the dust settle."

I knew exactly what he meant. On Saturday a thirty-storey mega-demon called Gordon the World-Eater had devastated the town centre. It was entirely possible that dust from disintegrated buildings still hung in the air after his rampage.

"But what about school?" said Zack.

Mum shot him a puzzled look. "Why the sudden interest in school, Luke?"

My brother had forgotten that he was in my body. He'd asked a question I would never raise. We were both going to have to look out for that pitfall. Thankfully, Mum let it pass. "I thought you knew – your school's been closed."

"Ofsted?"

"No," said Mum. "Freeze-ray."

She explained that a stray blast from Gordon the World-Eater had struck the school, transforming it into a massive ice cube. The official assessment was that the building would take a week to thaw out. Brilliant! However, it didn't alter the dire fact that we were leaving town. That was unfortunate. Because of Star Lad's presence, our hometown had become ground zero for interdimensional monster incursions and alien attacks. It would be just typical if another one happened while I was away.

"But we can't afford to go on holiday," I said. "You put all our money into the comic shop."

Dad nodded. "That's the best part – the trip isn't going to cost us a penny." He held up a voucher edged in gold and began to read the curly script printed across the front. "Congratulations, Parker family. In light of the recent destruction caused to your town by the sudden appearance of a giant, angry interdimensional being, we would like to invite you to relax, recover and reinvigorate at the south-west's most thought-provoking vacation destination. Over the coming weeks we hope to help as many families as possible from your neighbourhood to enjoy an all-inclusive, mindful mini-break at Great Minds Leisure Park."

"Never heard of it." I thought I knew all the major theme parks, but this one had passed me by. I took the brochure from Dad. Beneath the name was its slogan: *You Think You're So Smart!* The "o" in "So" had been replaced by a logo, which at first I took to be two halves of cauliflower stuck together, but then saw was in fact an illustration of a brain. With a sinking feeling I flicked through the rest of the brochure. Ten minutes ago I had hoped to embark on a hazardous mission requiring my new superpowers. Now it looked like the only thing I'd

be embarking on was a boring car journey to a theme park designed for the kind of kid who loves crosswords and brainteasers.

"This place looks amazing," said Zack with sickening enthusiasm. "Great Minds, here we come!"

2
PUGS IN HATS

"Fascinating," said Lara, studying me intently. "You're Zack on the outside but Luke on the inside."

"You are like a delicious filling." Serge sat close beside her on the floor of her bedroom.

We had gathered at Lara's house, two doors down from mine on Moore Street, to hold an emergency meeting of the Superhero Covert Alliance Reaction Force (S.C.A.R.F.) and discuss the ramifications (which meant *consequences* and not, as Lara was convinced, little castles built to protect medieval sheep from rustlers). As well as being the word-mangling Lara Lee she was also Dark Flutter, one of only two superheroes in the world.

Not that you could tell by looking around her disarmingly ordinary bedroom. She hid her secret identity well. Then again, if my major power was the ability to command small, mostly furry, animals, I'd keep it a secret too.

As my friends scrutinised my surprising appearance, I took the opportunity to study them. Without their help I'd never have returned safely from the parallel universe. There was a moment when I was sure I wouldn't make it back – in comics and films people are always getting lost in time and space. And in a way this world *was* different from the one I'd left a few days ago. The big change was that Serge and Lara were holding hands and finishing each other's sentences. It seemed as if Zack and I weren't the only ones who had exchanged brains. Serge and Lara were what I am reliably informed is called "an item". Which, it turns out, is not the same as an unexpected item in the bagging area but means they're going out together. Since returning I'd managed to grab two minutes alone with Serge and he had assured me that their togetherness hadn't yet progressed as far as matching pencil cases. Whatever that meant.

"What does it feel like?" Lara asked, her eyes big with wonder.

"You tell me," I replied. "You're the one with the boyf— Oh, you mean this." I brushed my adolescent arm. "Hairy."

She pulled a face, as if I'd provided an unsatisfactory answer.

"But you know the worst part?" I said.

She leaned in and in a low voice said, "The mind-bending terror of being separated from yourself, adrift in a body that's not your own, cast into a void of identity loss?"

"The casual wear!" said Serge with a snap of his fingers.

"Exactly!" I tugged at the sorry example of a T-shirt I'd been forced to put on that morning. It was blue. That was as much as anyone could say about it. "Zack doesn't own a single piece of clothing with a comic-related image or slogan."

"What about his Star Lad costume?" said Lara.

"That's different," I said, although she had a point. The thought made me tingle – the costume was mine to wear just as soon as I had a reason to don it. (You never just "put on" a superhero costume. You have to *don* one.) However, with no mission from Zorbon I had yet to find a valid excuse. And the costume didn't forgive the rest of Zack's questionable clothes.

"Ah, but if you have to put up with his dodgy wardrobe at least there is one major compensating factor, *oui*?"

Serge waggled his eyebrows.

He meant the superpowers.

Now, this was awkward. Naturally, I had attempted to try out my new powers at the earliest opportunity. Unfortunately, so far all I'd managed to do was use my telekinesis to move a pair of pants on the washing line, and if I'm honest I think that might have been the wind. For some reason I could not as yet access any of my brother's powers. I could feel them trapped inside me like a sneeze that won't come. It was unbearable.

"How about *un petit* demonstration?" asked Serge eagerly.

I should just have told him about my sad predicament but I was too embarrassed. If my comically challenged brother could leap tall buildings in a single bound, why couldn't I? I had a suspicion about what was happening inside me. I'd looked it up online. The brain has to be able to send and receive signals to things like muscles or glands in order to make them function. I supposed that's what superpowers must be like. Which meant that I was adapting to my new body, making fresh connections. Plugging in, basically. The problem was I'd been in Zack's body for less than twenty-four hours, but as soon as my synapses were firing on all cylinders I was sure I'd be up, up and away.

"It wouldn't be appropriate to use my new abilities for no reason," I lied. "With great power comes, y'know."

"That's very sensible of you," said Lara. "You seem more mature than before."

"That might be the hairy arms," I said.

She gave a small sigh. "So why are we at my house? S.C.A.R.F. meetings always take place at yours."

We had relocated for a very good reason. "I had to escape my brother," I explained.

"Has he turned evil?" asked Serge.

"In a manner of speaking. He's become so paranoid about the possibility of me sitting his exams that he's concocted a crazy back-up plan."

Serge's eyes widened. "Does it involve the Large Hadron Collider?"

What Zack had in mind was much worse than meddling with experimental particle physics under a mountain. "If he isn't back in his own body by the time his exams come around, he wants *me* to be ready to ace his maths GCSE." I let them absorb the full horror of my statement. "Zack intends to inflict a super-intensive study plan on me. He's in my body, and out of his mind."

"Who knows, it could be interesting," said Lara. "You might learn something."

"Maths, Lara. *Maths.*"

"Well, at least this way you and Zack will get to spend lots of time together," she went on. "That'll be nice."

I gestured to my borrowed body. "Uh, I think we're close enough, don't you?"

I filled them in on what Zorbon had told me about my situation. Not that I had much information to impart.

"Then all we can do is wait," said Serge when I'd finished.

"Not necessarily," said Lara. "Zorbon said that the reversal could be triggered by silence and stillness, right? I have an idea."

She headed out of the room. Serge and I followed her across the landing to another door, which shook with pounding music coming from the other side. Lara hammered on the door.

"Cara!"

"What?" came a reluctant answering call.

"I need to talk to you about meditation."

The song reached a particularly loud section.

"WHAT?!"

"MEDITATION!"

The music faded as the volume was turned down and a moment later the door flew open. Lara's big sister, Cara, stood on the threshold sporting the standard-issue older sibling expression of: *why are you bothering me, insignificant second child, I'm busy*. Cara's irritation was normal, but something about her seemed different. It took me a second to realise that it wasn't her, it was me. My perspective, to be exact. Instead of looking up at her from my usual height, we were almost at eye level.

She gave me a puzzled look. "What are *you* doing here?"

"Just hanging out."

"With my little sister?"

I felt a sudden pressure on my foot. Lara was standing on it. Now, why would she do something like— *Oh*. "I'm Zack," I blurted.

"Yeah, I know who you are." Cara frowned. "Are you OK?"

"No, he's not," said Lara, before I dug myself deeper into a hole. "That's what I wanted to talk to you about. Zack's, uh ... not feeling himself, and in order to get back to his old self he needs to relax. I thought you could help by teaching him to meditate." Lara turned to me. "Cara went on a course last year: Meditation and Entitlement."

"Enlightenment," Cara corrected her.

In truth I wasn't in a rush to get back to my old self. There was the small matter of first mastering Zack's superpowers.

"Don't worry about it," I said to Cara. "You're

obviously very busy listening to Billy Dark playlists and..." I leaned around her to squint into the bedroom. "Looking at posters of wolves with inspirational quotes."

"Ah, they are not all wolves," added Serge, craning his neck. "I also see a pug in a top hat with an uplifting couplet concerning self-worth."

Cara took a sideways step to block our view and folded her arms. "Y'know what, I *will* help you, Zack. I've seen you at school – I can't think of anyone who could do with learning to relax more than you." Her voice said "sympathy" but her face said "weirdo". "But I can't do anything for the next few days. We're going away."

What a relief. "That's all right. So are we." I'd persuaded Zack to hold off on the maths tuition until we returned from our holiday.

"*Et moi aussi*," Serge added. "My *maman* and I are soon to depart on our vacation."

All three families taking a holiday at the same time. That could mean only one thing.

"You're not going to Great Minds, by any chance?" I asked.

"*Oui*."

"Us too," said Lara.

"Oh great." Cara regarded us with dismay. "You're all coming on my mini-break." Grumbling to herself, she stepped back into her room and slammed the door in our faces.

Something inside me tingled with anticipation. Could it be Zack's superpowers warning me that our invitations were no coincidence? I looked round at my fellow members of S.C.A.R.F. and wondered what lay in store for us at Great Minds Leisure Park.

3
STAR SQUAD SIX

Before leaving to go on holiday I had an appointment to keep. Strictly speaking it was Zack's appointment, but under the current circumstances that meant me.

"Star Squad Six want to debrief me following Gordon the World-Eater's rampage," explained Zack as we headed into town on the bus.

Star Squad was a branch of the military set up to support Star Lad in times of global crisis. There were fast-reaction brigades stationed across the country; the one nearest us was number six. All I knew about them was that their mission aims seemed suspiciously like S.C.A.R.F.'s. I'd complained to Zack that there wasn't room for two identical organisations. We'd be competing for his attention, which would make for an inefficient use of his resources. He'd just pulled a face and said, "Yeah, S.C.A.R.F. and Star Squad are identical. Except that they have multi-role strike fighters, and a research and development budget they probably don't keep in a biscuit tin."

It was a cake tin, not a biscuit tin, but I was too miffed to correct him. The bus diverted from its usual route, avoiding cordoned streets damaged during the weekend's devastating battle. As it rumbled through less familiar parts of Bromley I felt my indignation replaced by excitement. Perhaps it would be cool to team up with a bunch of super-secret Spec Ops (that's short for Special Operations) in order to combat global threats. By the time we'd reached the shattered High Street I was on board with the whole idea.

"So where's the meeting?" I asked. "No, don't tell me. Underground HQ with alpha-level security? Sub-orbital stealth airship?"

"We usually meet at the Civic Centre," said Zack. "It's very central. Easy for everyone to get to and there's the multistorey car park. I'll be waiting outside afterwards."

"Aren't you coming?"

"They don't know my real identity, so if the two of us

show up…"

"Say no more," I said, tapping a finger against my nose. "Batman never tells Commissioner Gordon that he's Bruce Wayne."

Zack wasn't quite finished. "Also, I'd have to explain about the body swap and that would be so embarrassing."

He hadn't hidden his disgust for the swap, which frankly I found insulting. "It's not that bad."

"Not for you," he said. "You got *my* body."

"Hey! What's wrong with mine?"

"Oh, let's see, shall we? For a start, you're short. I can barely reach the kitchen cupboards now. Your feet are wonky – even with the orthotics in your shoes it's tough to walk straight. Also, make a note, when we swap back you need to get your eyes tested. What else, apart from the physical downsides? Most of your shoes light up. That's just … off. Then there are your clothes. Do you own *anything* without a superhero character splashed across it?" He pulled at his trouser-waist and peered into the gap. "Even your pants are themed."

I caught a flash of the Flash.

"But most of all, Luke, I've been eleven." He heaved a great sigh. "I don't need to go through it again."

The bus came to a stop and we disembarked. Five minutes later I found myself in a loo in McDonald's (the one not flattened when the Glades Shopping Centre was trampled), donning my superhero costume for the first time. As I smoothed the star-flecked tunic across my chest I reflected that in my life I must have occupied dozens of bathroom cubicles in order to don a mask and cape. However, on those occasions I had merely been playing at superheroes: preparing for a party, dressing up for Halloween, getting through a slow Thursday. Today was different. Finally, I slid the mask down over my eyes, stepped out of the cubicle and admired myself in the bathroom mirror.

I. Was. Star Lad.

OK, it was Zack's body I was in, and Zack's eyes I looked through, and despite a lot of practising I hadn't yet managed to muster a single superpower. But I couldn't help it, I did a little happy dance, shimmying my hips, tapping my heroically booted feet on the tiled floor and chanting, "I'm Star Lad. I'm Star Lad. I'm Star Lad. I'm Star—"

Zack coughed. He stood guarding the door, preventing anyone from coming in and witnessing my quick-change. "You done?"

Almost.

After a last-minute wee and a sneaky McMuffin we headed out. I had to sign a few autographs on the way to

the Civic Centre, which was cool. Everyone wanted to talk to Star Lad and have their picture taken. Zack and I made sure not to be photographed together, to avoid the risk of anyone identifying us as brothers. We reached our destination and ducked down an alley, out of sight of curious passers-by.

"You'll be meeting my liaison, Colonel Crowe," said Zack. "He's in charge of Star Squad. I'll describe him so you'll know who to expect."

"No need. I expect he has an eyepatch like Nick Fury's."

"He does not and, before you ask, no I don't know who Nick Fury is and—" He held up a finger to stall my explanation. "I don't care. Now, just listen. These are serious people and they're going to treat you with respect and *gravitas*. So try not to say anything stupid. That means no talking about comics. Above all, remember you're Star Lad."

It was the first time my brother had acknowledged our role reversal. I grinned inwardly.

"Stop grinning."

OK, maybe not so much *inwardly*.

"Also, if my previous meetings are anything to go by," Zack continued, "Star Squad may well have some new equipment for you. Last time they gave me that emergency starlight recharger."

I gasped. "I'm going to get gadgets! This is like James Bond!" I gripped his arm. "I bet they give me an Aston Martin."

He shook me off. "It will not be an Aston Martin."

"You don't know that."

Zack sighed. "Whatever they give you, just promise me you won't immediately start fiddling with it. If you break their special equipment—"

"I won't," I protested.

"Yeah," he muttered. "Just like you *didn't* break my headphones."

I caught his accusing glare – it was definitely time for me to be on my way.

I sat alone in the Bluebell Room, one of the Civic Centre's four public meeting rooms, waiting for Star Squad Six to show. According to the council information leaflet I'd picked up, the room was available weekdays (mornings only), and for a hire fee of £130 provided seating for six and use of a CD player. I slotted the leaflet back in its plastic holder on the desk and sat back. I kicked my heels and waited some more. So far the only person I'd seen was a technician from the council's IT department with a briefing on the correct use of the CD player.

There was the sound of clipped footsteps from outside in the corridor, the door swung open and in marched a surprisingly short figure wearing an army uniform consisting of black leather boots, khaki trousers and jacket, and a navy beret sporting the distinctive Star Squad insignia of a mask and cape surrounded by exploding stars. So big was the beret in proportion to his head that the brim had fallen down over his eyes. He pushed it up with a finger, revealing the face of a boy, perhaps six or seven years old.

I stared. "Colonel Crowe?"

"Sorry, Star Lad," said a grown-up voice behind him, and into the room came a harassed-looking man in an identical uniform to the boy's. He fitted Zack's description of the colonel. He shot a look at the boy. "Colin, I told you to wait."

"Sorry, Dad," mumbled the boy without taking his eyes off me.

"Apologies, Star Lad, but it's Bring-Your-Child-To-Work-Day and when young Colin here heard I was meeting you, well, I'm sure you can understand. He's a big fan."

"I can't believe it," said Colin, his eyes round with wonder. "Is it really you?"

Um, not exactly, I thought to myself. Thankfully,

before I had to lie to his face his dad interrupted.

"I told you on the way over," he said in a low voice. "This is Daddy's debriefing session. Have you got your crisps?" Colin nodded, holding up a packet of Wotsits. "OK, then just sit down over there and don't interrupt."

Colin did as he was told, climbing on to one of the Bluebell Room's six chairs and noisily opening his crisps. With his son settled, the colonel took a deep breath and turned to me. He clutched a ribbed metal briefcase, which he proceeded to set down on the desk.

"Very well," he said. "Time to get down to business." He sprung the catches on the briefcase and opened the lid.

Gadgets! Now we were talking.

"I know what you're thinking," he said.

"That briefcase isn't big enough for an Aston Martin?"

He looked confused. "Uh, I was referring to the recall notice? Did you bring the starlight recharger?"

I fished it out. This credit card-sized device had got Star Lad out of a tight spot during our latest adventure.

"Thank you, I'll take that." He plucked it out of my hands.

"But what if I need it again?"

"Afraid not. Under certain conditions we've determined that the installed battery can explode."

"Like a dodgy phone?"

"More like a supernova." Holding it gingerly between thumb and forefinger, Colonel Crowe lowered the charger into a hazardous-waste bag, sealed it up and placed it in the case. "We're dealing with experimental technology – there are bound to be teething problems."

The rustle of a crisp packet came from the other side of the room.

"Colin," said his dad in a warning tone.

I craned my neck to peer into the briefcase. "So what *have* you got for me? Wristwatch with a laser, flamethrower disguised as bagpipes, jetpack?"

"What do you want with a jetpack? You can fly!"

"Oh yeah."

"Dad, Dad," said Colin, unable to contain his excitement one moment longer. "Can I show him? *Please*."

In his long military career Colonel Crowe had probably faced down lots of fearsome foes but this was one opponent he couldn't resist. "Fine," he said grudgingly.

Colin needed no more invitation. He hopped down from the chair and scampered over, snatching the briefcase from his dad.

"Wait till you see this, Star Lad," he said, digging in

the case.

I noticed that his lips were smeared with orange Wotsit dust and when he spoke there was a waft of cheese. Before he could reveal whatever he was so keen to show me, there was a tentative knock at the door.

"Ah, excuse me." There stood a red-faced man wearing a rumpled suit and a tie with a fish pattern. "Barry Lodge, from the council. Sorry to interrupt, only we've a slight problem with the room hire. Your card didn't go through." He held out a credit-card machine.

Grumbling at the interruption, the colonel went to sort out the problem, leaving me alone with Colin.

"Here they are!" he said, pulling a pair of trainers from the case.

They were the kind of trainers that you colour in yourself. You start with a pair of blank white shoes and use special pens to draw on them. At first glance they looked perfectly normal but this was Star Squad, so there had to be more to them than met the eye.

"So what are they packing?" I asked. "Dart gun in the toe? Quantum lock-pick in the heel? Or, if you pull the lace a certain way, do they transform into a mini-submarine?"

"No, but I coloured them in myself," said Colin. "See, I did a drawing of the Nemesis asteroid here, the alien

mothership on this one, here's the giant monster-thing and this is your sigil on the toe." He offered them to me. "You're my favourite superhero – I wanted to give you something."

I struggled to come to terms with what was on offer. "So ... they're just shoes?"

He nodded.

That was disappointing. And it wasn't as if the drawings were much good. "Do they light up?"

Colin shook his head sadly. I had let him down with my reaction. The trainers *were* a thoughtful touch and at least they were better than anything currently in Zack's wardrobe. I thanked him, but that wasn't the end of it.

"I gave you something," said Colin. "Now it's your turn. Do one of your superpowers. Fly round the room. No, no, wait – make *me* fly using telekinesis."

He looked at me expectantly. Even if I'd wanted to show off, I couldn't do either of those things. Was I about to be rumbled by Colin Crowe? Thankfully, just then the colonel returned.

"Very well," he said, having sorted the problem with the room hire. "Shall we begin?" He shooed his son back to the corner of the room and Colin returned to his swivel chair.

I prepared to answer the colonel's questions but

I couldn't tear my eyes away from the scribbled-on trainers. My life was so unfair. It seemed every time Zack got a cool present – like a phone, or superpowers – I always ended up with the same thing. Shoes.

4
AN UNEXPECTED SOJOURN-EY

"Strap yourselves in," said Dad. "I'm about to make the jump to light sp—"

"I think I forgot to water the yucca," muttered Mum, unbuckling her seatbelt and darting out of the car.

Sadly, Dad was making one of his lame jokes. Our car didn't have a hyperspace engine. So instead of reaching our destination in a matter of seconds through a swirling tunnel of folded space, we sat in our driveway poised to embark on a five-and-a-half-hour trek that would take in the delights of the M3, A303 and, according to Google Maps, four sets of major roadworks. And with a roofbox and two mountain bikes strapped to the boot, we were unlikely to worry the national speed limit, never mind the Kessel Run record. On the other hand, I'd worked out that were I able to use Zack's flying power I could make it to Great Minds in three minutes flat. Of course, that was not an option. Instead, my fate was to be cooped up in the car, unable to experiment with any of Zack's superpowers, and with nothing to distract me except for *The Big Bumper Book of Crosswords* and the lingering threat of a Paddington Bear audiobook. (Dad had ended his audiobook subscription six years ago, immediately after the free trial expired, leaving us with a severely limited choice.)

"I sense a disturbance in the Force," Dad said, turning round in his seat. "Zack, why is Luke playing with your phone?"

We had swapped bodies but not possessions. Normally I wasn't allowed near his precious phone. Or, I should say, *Luke* wasn't allowed. Which gave me a perfect opportunity.

"Give it over, squirt," I said, extending a hand.

An expression of alarm spread across my brother's face. "What? No way."

"Now, Luke," said Dad. "It's your brother's phone. When you're old enough then you'll get one of your own, *if* you've earned it."

Unable to object, he thrust the phone at me. Folding his arms tightly across his chest, he threw himself back into the seat with a grunt of stifled rage.

Maybe this journey wouldn't be so bad after all.

Mum returned from watering her plant and she wasn't alone. To my surprise, beside her stood Serge, wearing what I think is called a cravat and with a monogrammed weekend bag slung casually over one shoulder. It transpired that Serge's *maman* had come down with a bug. The upshot of which was that he was coming with us. Bad for her, great for me. He stowed his bag in the boot and slid into the back seat between Zack and me. We greeted each other excitedly.

"When we get there, can Serge and I share a room?" I asked my parents.

Mum gave me a puzzled look. "Zack, why would you want to share with Serge?"

I kept forgetting that to the outside world I was Zack, not Luke.

"Yeah, Serge is *my* friend," said my brother with a mischievous grin. "I'll share a room with him. You need lots of peace and quiet – to study for your exams."

The sneaky little—

"And don't worry, *Zack*," he went on. "No one expects you to join in any of the childish fun and games, ride the amazing rollercoaster or take a refreshing dip in the water park." He placed a hand over his heart. "And I promise not to disturb you with our shrieks of joy."

Mum and Dad exchanged baffled looks. "Serge, any chance Luke has been replaced by a charming and considerate robot double?" asked Dad.

"These days," said Serge, pursing his lips, "there is always that chance."

With a clatter from the engine and a crunch of gears, we set off on our long journey into the west. We were like the last of the Elves at the end of their time on Middle-earth, but with a car picnic. It didn't take long to join the motorway, but we'd barely made any progress when an overhead sign warned of queues ahead and soon we were bogged down in traffic. Mum cracked open the picnic to avoid what she called "dissent in the ranks". Five sausage rolls and a Thermos of hot chocolate later, the traffic had eased enough for Dad to press on.

The miles didn't exactly fly by but at last we began to eat into the journey. Concrete gave way to glimpses of open fields. Zack gazed out of the window but I could tell he wasn't interested in the scenery. He was still moping about being stuck in my body. And then – miraculously – we were halfway. With the prospect of our holiday closer than ever, Serge consulted the Great

Minds activities brochure.

"I have already signed us up for the brain-food baking class," he said.

What was he thinking? "I don't want to do that."

"Ah, not *us*. I meant Lara and me. She makes a superb Genoise."

"Oh yeah." I kept forgetting that they were an *item*. But they weren't just any plain old couple. I lowered my voice to make sure Mum and Dad couldn't overhear, but it probably wasn't necessary over their tuneless singalong to "Avalon" by Bryan Ferry. "What's it like going out with, y'know?"

"A girl?"

Sometimes I… "A *superhero*."

Serge cocked his head. "I had not really thought about it. She has always been Lara to me."

It seemed to me he was missing out on an opportunity to learn the truth "behind the mask". "What do you two talk about?"

He shrugged. "The same stuff you and I talk about. Also baking." He paused. "And the future."

"What, you mean robot swarms and space elevators?"

"No," he replied. "I mean growing up."

"Oh, that." These days it always seemed to come back to that.

"But I should be asking you." He gestured to my temporary body. "You have been to the future. So what have you to report from the brave new world? What is it like being fourteen?"

I hadn't really considered it until he asked. Zack was super-smart and super-fit and super-you-know-what. He was on the fast track to a future full of good things. Even if his life was made slightly less perfect by the fact that his dream girl, Cara, hadn't yet noticed him. So what was the view like from here? I was struck by a surprising answer. I realised that most of all I just wanted to be me again. That couldn't be right, could it?

Zack leaned over. "What are you two talking about?"

"Robot swarms," I said, shooting Serge a look.

"And space elevators," he added.

Mercifully, the parental singing stopped. Dad glanced in his rear-view mirror.

"If this idiot in the white van gets any closer he'll be in our boot."

It wasn't a van, it was one of those motorhomes you could live in. We were being harassed by a vehicle with a toilet.

"I could use my force field to keep him off," I whispered to Serge. I still hadn't mastered any of my powers but it was worth a shot.

Zack sent me a warning glare. I pressed myself back into my seat with a huff. This was agonising, being stuck in the car unable to do anything.

"Patience, *mon ami*," said Serge, patting my knee. "I feel certain we will require your new-found abilities during our unexpected *sojourn*."

I didn't know what a sojourn was, but I figured it must be like a holiday. Serge and I had already discussed the coincidence of our invitations with Lara, back at her house. It had seemed to me there were two possibilities. One – the invitations were genuine. But Serge had said that coincidences like that didn't happen. Not in Bromley. I tended to agree with him. That left option number two, in which—

"An evil, hyperintelligent blancmange is masterminding a plot to bring about the end of the world," Serge had suggested.

"And why a blancmange, specifically?" Lara had asked. "Just curious."

Serge waved a hand. "*Ah*, my proposal is not dependent on a blancmange."

"Oh good."

"It could be any kind of gelatinous sweet dessert. A sinister panna cotta or—"

"I feel you may be jumping a few steps," said Lara.

"And you're ignoring the big question."

"What does the evil pudding want with us?" I figured that's what she meant.

Lara let out a long sigh.

I sensed that she wasn't convinced by Serge's theory, but if my recent adventures had taught me anything, it was the importance of keeping an open mind. Once we reached our destination we'd be in a better position to uncover the exact flavour and consistency of the threat. If any. I really hoped there was one – I needed something to get my superpowered teeth into. As soon as I got the hang of Zack's powers, I'd use his Star-Sense to detect any danger, and I was confident there'd be enough wildlife at the place for Lara to set up early-warning squirrels.

We'd wound up the meeting with a disagreement over which colour of alert the situation called for. Serge wanted to go full-on Red, but Lara felt strongly that though caution was called for we weren't in any immediate danger, so Orange would be more appropriate. In the end we compromised.

S.C.A.R.F. was officially at Threat Level Salmon.

A gazillion years later we made a brief stop at some motorway services for a wee. When I returned to the car I passed the area reserved for larger vehicles, and I

was sure I saw the motorhome that had tried to overtake us earlier. Could it be following us? The driver sat at the wheel, but the sun was in my eyes and even when I squinted I couldn't make out any more than a silhouette. Dad called on me to hurry up, and it was time to go. Back on the road I kept an eye out for the mysterious motorhome, but I didn't see it again.

The journey dragged on. We resorted to playing a game of I Don't Spy, the variation on the classic time-waster, which allows you to choose any object in the universe rather than be limited to Tree, Cloud, or Back-of-Dad's-Head. That killed eight minutes. Surely there was some way to make this tedious journey pass more quickly.

"I believe it's time," Dad said, reaching for the audio controls, "for Paddington!"

The sun was setting when we finally passed through the gates of Great Minds Leisure Park. The name was emblazoned in metre-high multicoloured bubble letters that spanned the gap between two stone pillars. The slogan slotted in beneath: *You Think You're So Clever!* Just as in the brochure, the "o" in "So" had been replaced by the park logo, but this one was super-sized.

"It's a giant brain," I muttered.

Dad pointed through the windscreen. "Wow! Do you see that?"

The resort sat atop a hill, a collection of soaring glass spires, golden domes and landing platforms, encircled by a spiralling monorail. The last rays of the sun lit up the topmost tower. It was the sort of incredible futuristic cityscape I could imagine designed by someone like, well, me.

However, as we drove closer we saw the truth. The megacity was a mega-fake – nothing more than a giant billboard. In the lower right-hand corner in suspiciously small print were the words: PHASE 2 – COMING SOON!

We crested the hill and rounded the advert. Dad stopped the car to take in the sight before us. Spread out along the length of a wooded valley floor was the actual resort.

It consisted of a single rollercoaster overgrown with weeds, one sad bouncy castle and a water slide that chuted into an outdoor pool filled with water a colour I'd only ever seen before in the boys' toilets at school. There was no shining monorail, just a fleet of what looked like golf buggies shuttling between a handful of grubby dome-shaped buildings. As for the accommodation, scattered among the trees were not the state-of-the-art living pods

promised in the brochure, but a series of static caravans. Birds circled high over the park. Possibly vultures.

"I suppose this must be Phase One," said Mum.

"Not exactly the Magic Kingdom, is it?" said Zack.

"More like the Tragic Kingdom," I muttered.

"Never mind," said Dad cheerfully. "Let's remember the most important thing."

"Family?"

"Minigolf?"

"It's free." Dad put the car in gear and we grumbled on.

Five minutes and an accidental detour later past Bird Brain, the bird-of-prey centre, we arrived outside the main reception building. It was one of those dome-shaped structures I'd seen from the hill. I'd like to say up close it was more impressive. But I can't. It was grey and slightly crumpled and looked like the cap my grandma wears to the swimming pool.

Mum and Dad went inside to check us in, while we unfolded ourselves from the car. I stretched my arms and let out a groan of relief. It was good to be upright again.

"I'm telling you that wasn't a hawk," I said. "It was a pigeon with stuck-on talons." Before I could lower my arms, there was a rustle from some nearby bushes and half a dozen commandos leapt out of the undergrowth, fanning out to surround us. Our ambushers were space marines, wearing combat armour in camouflage colours, presumably complete with life-support technology to cope with hostile atmospheres, and helmets containing sophisticated targeting systems. Each squad member gripped a tactical pulse rifle.

"I was expecting shenanigans," whispered Serge, "but hoped I would first get to sample the continental breakfast."

So much for my S.C.A.R.F. readiness alert – I'd walked straight into a trap. Worse than that, standing there with my hands up, I had arrived pre-surrendered.

The leader took a step forward and pointed his weapon at Zack.

"Luke Parker," his voice rasped through his helmet respirator. "Prepare to be atomised!"

5
THE SADDEST PANCAKE IN THE WORLD

I froze, helpless before the heavily armed troops.

"Quick, use your powers," Serge urged me in a whisper.

Zack's powers had appeared in a time of great need. *Come the hour, come the Lad.* Perhaps this was my moment. The frustrating part was I knew precisely what to do. First, I'd encircle everyone with a protective force field, next I'd disarm the leader with my telekinetic power, then I'd round them up and fly them to the nearest police station. "Don't mention it, officer. Just doing my duty."

Here goes, I thought to myself, and stuck out

both hands. "Force field, force field, force field..." I mumbled over and over, willing one to appear. Sadly, nothing materialised. However, the space marines were so distracted by my mad hand actions and mumbling that they took their eye off my brother. In that moment he took a step towards the leader and reached for his weapon. The fool! He was going to get himself atomised.

"Ha-ha, very funny," he said. "Now, put that thing down before someone gets—"

There was a pop from the barrel and a green splodge of paint appeared on my brother's chest (ruining one of *my* favourite Superman sweatshirts). With a chuckle the leader removed his helmet.

"Gotcha, Luke-*a-saurus*!"

I gawped at the figure standing before me. "Josh?"

With a puzzled expression Joshpal Khan turned his attention from the boy he thought was Luke, to me. Josh had helped out during our latest adventure with my Evil Twin, and Lara had proposed making him an "anti-social member" of S.C.A.R.F. I think she meant "associate member", although she had a point.

"That wasn't funny," complained Zack, pinching the smeared sweatshirt. "Paintball guns should never be fired in such proximity, and never at someone without eye protection."

"You what?" Josh was clearly baffled as to why I had suddenly turned into a humourless stick-in-the-mud.

"What are you doing here?" I quizzed him.

He turned to me, puzzled as to why he was being addressed by Zack, someone he barely knew, while Luke stood off, stand-offishly.

"Uh, we all got this free invitation," Josh explained. At this the other marines removed their helmets, revealing themselves to be yet more of my classmates. There were a chorus of "hi"s from Henry Chapman, Hugo Hill, Evie Stansfield, and That Kid from my physics class whose name I can never remember.

"Hmm," Serge mused. "What could the evil blancmange possibly want with all of them?"

I could see Josh begin to form a question, then give up. "Loads of our year are here. It's like the best school trip ever."

"No it isn't, this place is awful," said Evie, with a curdled expression. "Most of the rides are broken, and the ones that work are rubbish. The only reason my parents didn't immediately turn around and leave is because the one thing in perfect working order is the adults-only spa."

"At least it's better than Centaur Park," protested Josh. "I didn't see *one* mythical creature."

Just then Mum and Dad returned, accompanied by a young woman wearing the staff uniform of a black blazer edged with silver piping, a black round-neck jumper, light-coloured trousers and shiny black shoes. As she drew closer I saw that she was wearing an ear-piece with a slim microphone wand that followed the curve of her cheek.

"Hello brain-boxes, and welcome to Great Minds!" She greeted us with outstretched arms. "I'm Sarah, your dedicated host for the duration of your stay." She indicated an oversized name badge pinned to her chest. It was in the shape of a brain and on it was written: *Sarah Pelham. Host.* "You must be Zack, Luke and Serge." She shook each of our hands in turn. As she came to me I caught a strong whiff of perfume. It nearly knocked me over.

"Are you ready to have a great time?" she asked.

We replied with a chorus of half-hearted yeses.

"Outstanding!" she said, handing each of us a purple rubber wristband. "Wear these at all times. The wristband contains a chip that lets the systems in the park know who you are and it'll give you free access to all the rides, free entry to the attractions, and free meals at all our dining experiences."

"Will it also give me free access to the doughnut

carts?" asked Serge.

"It certainly will," said Sarah.

"But, Serge, your *maman* told me to keep an eye on your snacking," Mum added.

Serge looked horrified. "But how can this be? She is always saying I am perfect just as I am."

While Serge reeled, Zack took the opportunity to retrieve his precious phone from me. Sarah noticed us wrestling over the handset.

"I wouldn't bother arguing about that," she said. "At Great Minds we believe in switching off, enjoying nature, and spending time with each other without the constant interruption from electronic devices. You'll find that your phones, tablets and laptops won't work here. There's no mobile signal and no Wi-Fi."

Either we were in a blackspot, or the park was operating some kind of electronic jamming. If so, that was suspicious for a leisure resort. As far as I knew you didn't get anything like that at Center Parcs.

"What a good idea," said Mum. She and Dad had the same weird, bright-eyed expression, like they were standing in front of a big church window. "A chance to talk to one another, face-to-face. Just be together."

Didn't bear thinking about. "Not all the time, though? Right?"

Dad scowled and unfolded a map of the resort. "Now, our living-pods—"

"Static caravans," corrected Zack.

Dad ignored him. "They're over here in … Mental Block 3. How do we get there, Sarah?"

"Let me show you," she began, but before she could explain further, Josh butted in.

"You need to take the Smug-Buggies," he said, squeezing on his wristband, which bleeped in response. "They'll be here in a minute."

Sarah beamed a smile. "Well, it's clear that you're in good hands. So if you'll excuse me." She threw us a wave and I got another whiff of that strong scent as she left. "Have a mind-blowing day!"

"Did you smell her perfume?" I asked when she'd gone and my head had cleared.

"Mmm," Serge nodded. "I would say it is a blend of patchouli, lavender and something else I cannot put my highly developed nose on."

Just as Josh predicted, the buggies arrived a minute later. They were designed to look like giant brains on wheels, a fleet of open-topped driverless vehicles that ferried guests around the park. At the front was the sensing technology that let the cars guide themselves along the paved pathways criss-crossing the resort. A

red scanning light swept back and forth like a constantly swivelling eye.

Josh, Serge and I climbed into the first buggy, while Zack, Mum and Dad took the one behind. As soon as I sat down a seatbelt zipped out of the door frame, wrapped itself across my chest and secured me in place with a boa constrictor-like squeeze. There was no steering wheel or dials on the dashboard, not even a touchscreen.

"Greetings," cooed a computerised voice. "I am the Highly Autonomous Land-vehicle 9000. The 9000 series have never jumped a red light or broken a speed limit. We are foolproof and incapable of error."

Josh threw me a look. "See what I mean? Smug."

"Please state your destination," said the vehicle.

I named the section of the resort and, with a whine from the electric motor, the buggy whisked us down the hill, weaving its way through the trees with unerring accuracy.

We passed through several different sectors, each labelled with a similarly themed title. Fore!head featured minigolf. Brain Freeze was the indoor ice-skating rink. Heads Up! was the treetop adventure walkway. We rolled past the hairdressing salon, which was just called The Hairdressing Salon. In each sector we met more of the resort's hosts, each dressed in a uniform like Sarah's.

They waved at us as we scooted by, offering up the same cheery wish that we "Have a mind-blowing day!" It was deeply irritating.

"I call them Blazers," said Josh. "Because they wear blazers."

It turned out that Josh and his family had been coming here for years, so when it came to the resort he was an expert. He warned me about the food.

"It's bad. I mean, seriously awful. Like, the cook has never met an actual human being. We always used to order out. For years this place was buzzing with takeaway delivery riders. Drove the Blazers bonkers. See, you're only supposed to eat at the resort restaurants. I think that's why they blocked the phone signal – to stop you calling out for pizza."

Josh rattled on with more useless information until at last the buggy deposited us at our destination.

"Please rate your driverless experience," said the 9000 series.

"Give it a ten," whispered Josh. "If you don't it gets huffy."

Josh was staying in another sector, called Sleepyhead. He remained in his seat and the Smug-Buggies departed, leaving us to move in to our new accommodation.

The caravan sat in a clearing next to two others. It

was long and narrow with a pitched roof and corrugated walls in a grubby cream colour. At one end was a bay window filled with washed-out net curtains, and on the wall beside the front door was a plaque with a name: The Monte Carlo.

"Why is it they're always named after places you'd rather be?" said Dad. Mum nudged him in the ribs.

We used to go on caravan holidays all the time. I remembered loving them when I was younger. The best bit was that I got to share a berth with Zack. (A berth is what you call a bed in a caravan and also a luxury yacht.) We would stay up late and have whispered conversations and eat Haribo. It was great.

"What a dump," moaned Zack.

"Luke," said Mum with a puzzled frown. "I thought you liked caravan holidays."

She shrugged off his complaint and we dragged our cases inside. She and Dad chose the biggest room with its own bathroom, while Serge and Zack shared a twin and I got my own, which I suspected might actually be a food cupboard. My suspicions were raised by an unopened tin of beans on the built-in shelves and a stack of old takeaway menus gathering dust in a drawer. The caravan also had a living room with an old-fashioned fireplace (fake), a galley kitchen and a second bathroom that smelled strongly of pine air freshener. We unpacked and then Dad suggested that since the only food in the place was the solitary tin of beans, we should go out for something to eat. We all agreed that was a great idea, except Zack, who was in a total huff. Serge was especially keen to sample the cuisine and had compiled a list of Great Minds' many restaurants in order of portion size. I didn't have the heart to pass on Josh's review of the resort's food offerings. Serge recommended somewhere called the Brainpan for pancakes, which according to the map lay on the other side of the resort. I was about to hail a Smug-Buggy using my wristband when one arrived.

"What are we even doing here?" Zack moaned. "I should be at home, studying. I could be at the library. Right now."

I could see that Mum and Dad were confused by this uncharacteristic outburst from what appeared to be their youngest son. If Zack didn't shut up soon, Dad really would believe that we'd swapped bodies.

Two passengers climbed out of the recently arrived buggy and made their way across the clearing towards us. It was Lara and Cara Lee.

At the sight of Cara, Zack instantly stopped complaining. Serge once told me that when someone has fancied someone else for a long time without that person

noticing, you say that they "hold a torch" for them. For Cara, Zack held the Mega-Nova 4000, which is the world's brightest torch.

"Hi, kid," she said to him, ruffling his hair. She always called me kid and there was a certain amount of hair-ruffling in our interaction, which didn't bother me, but I could tell that Zack wasn't keen. More than anything he wanted Cara to notice him. But not like this.

"I'm not a kid, I'm a..." He tailed off, mumbling dismally. "Kid."

It turned out that the girls were staying in the caravan next to ours. They were our neighbours, just like back home.

"Where's your mum?" asked Mum.

"The spa," said Cara.

"We got here this morning," said Lara. "And apart from a quick bite at the Brainpan she's been there ever since."

"Sounds like my kind of place," said Mum.

"It's not fair – they don't allow anyone in under the age of eighteen," complained Cara.

"As I was saying," smiled Mum.

"So what about you – where have you been?" I gave Lara a meaningful stare. "Seen anything ... interesting?" I wondered if she'd had a chance to reconnoitre the place and discover any of its secrets.

"The pancakes," she said, "are sad."

Must be a coded message. Of course, what was I thinking? She couldn't pass on sensitive information in front of non-S.C.A.R.F. members.

I nodded slowly at her. "We should discuss 'the sad pancakes' later."

"Uh, OK," she said.

I felt a hand on my arm. It belonged to Cara.

"You and me," she said. "Yoga class, noon tomorrow at the Mindfulness Activity Centre."

"What?!" blurted Zack.

"Shh, Luke," said Dad. "Cara and Zack are talking."

"Omigod, why is she asking *him*? This is... I can't even..."

"You said you wanted stillness and inner calm," said Cara. "Here's your chance."

I had an investigation to carry out and no time for such distractions. However, I couldn't just point-blank refuse her invitation, I had to come up with a believable excuse. "Can't, I'm afraid. I've got a Dungeons and Dragons pottery class booked at the same time."

"NO!" shrieked Zack. He stomped back inside the caravan, slamming the flimsy door behind him.

Cara shot me a look of confusion and pity. "Well, if

you change your mind, I'll be there. Come on, sis, we have to get changed for the Billy Dark concert."

"Billy Dark is playing at Great Minds?" I asked, somewhat surprised. It didn't seem like the kind of venue where you would find one of the most popular acts in the country.

"Not Billy Dark," said Cara, without any loss of enthusiasm. "Billy *Darque*. He's a tribute act."

"The third-best tribute act in the south-west," Lara added, before turning to Serge. "I got you a ticket."

Serge put a hand to his heart. "Such a thoughtful gesture."

Lara shrugged. "They were free."

The two girls headed next door to their caravan to get ready for the concert, while we retrieved an incoherent Zack and made our way to the Brainpan.

When the meal arrived I discovered that Lara's message had not been coded after all. It wasn't only the pancakes that were sad, the whole place reeked of griddled regret. It was the saddest pancake restaurant in the world. Our disappointing dinner churning in our bellies, we went our separate ways. Serge and Mum joined Lara and Cara at the concert while Dad, Zack and I swung by the indoor tennis courts. There was a sign on the door informing us that due to adverse weather conditions the courts were closed. Dad shook his head, mystified. "But they're *inside*."

We returned to the caravan for the night, and as the Smug-Buggy dropped us off I reminded myself that this holiday wasn't about indoor tennis. I was on a mission. Of sorts. Tomorrow S.C.A.R.F. would commence a full sweep of the resort. If something was going on here, we'd uncover it in the course of the day. Serge also wanted to make time for minigolf, and Zack had expressed an interest in Mount Cleverest, the combination indoor climbing wall and maths maze. I really hoped that Great Minds was more than it seemed: an ordinary, if rather terrible, holiday resort.

An hour and a half of angry Cluedo later, I headed for bed. I passed the open door to Zack and Serge's room. Through it I could see two narrow beds. It was obvious which one was Serge's. On the shelf on his side sat a neat row of bottles. From experience I knew it was a selection of moisturisers, lotions and scents for every occasion. He took them everywhere, even on camping trips. I felt a pang of envy. Sure, my best friend was a bit eccentric, but *I* should be sharing a room with him, not my brother. It wasn't fair. Reluctantly, I settled down to sleep in my honest-it's-not-the-larder. I was just nodding off when I was disturbed by a rustling from outside. I assumed

it was Mum and Serge returning from the concert, but when after a minute I didn't hear the click of the front door I decided to take a look. Kneeling up on the bed I peered out to see a shadowy shape in the undergrowth on the edge of the clearing. Someone was sneaking around our caravan. Curious to discover the identity of the intruder, I left my berth and crept to the front door. Opening it so as not to disturb the other occupants, I went outside.

A fake old-timey lantern stuck to the outside of the caravan cast a ring of light. Standing just outside the reach of its glow lurked the figure, legs shoulder-width apart, knees slightly bent, shoulders relaxed. She stepped into the light.

It was Miss Dunham, my former gym teacher.

She wore dark-coloured tracksuit bottoms, a white vest and a white towelling headband. Her bare arms were musclier than I remembered. In the pale light I could make out the expression on her face. She looked even more serious than that time I'd mistaken her for a supervillain and trapped her in a hockey goal.

She held out a hand.

"Come with me if you want to live to see your next birthday."

6
POST-GYMNASTIC STRESS

My recent confrontation with an Alien Overlord in the school gym had left me shaken, but it had affected Miss Dunham even more. She had witnessed the alien's horrifying attempt to make me a lunchtime snack, and the very next day had taken an extended leave of absence. The official explanation was that she'd left for unspecified health reasons. The rumour among my schoolmates was that she had taken one too many dodgeballs to the head. Only S.C.A.R.F. knew the truth. I had a feeling that her experience would explain why she was turning up outside people's caravans in the middle of the night spouting ominous declarations about birthdays.

However, my first thought was that the person standing in front of me was not in fact Miss Dunham. My reasoning was ruthlessly logical. When aliens had attempted to invade Earth, they had taken on the identity of my terrifying gym teacher.

I had to assume that she was one of them, and all of this was a trick.

Far from being scared, I was curious. And being prepared was half the battle. Knowing that, I followed the so-called Miss Dunham away from the caravan and into the undergrowth. It would have been easier to travel on the walkways that crossed the resort, but at her insistence we kept off the well-lit paths.

"Surveillance cameras," she whispered, "watching every move we make."

She cut a swathe through bushes and brambles, confidently navigating her way in the darkness. Suddenly she crouched down, pulling me with her. She put a finger to her lips and nodded towards the path, where one of the Smug-Buggies glided past, its red scanning light glowing through the trees. She waited for it to trundle out of sight before signalling for us to continue our journey.

A short time later we arrived at our destination: a quiet, out-of-the-way spot on the very edge of the resort. Parked next to a small pond, screened by trees, was the motorhome that had tailed us earlier that day.

"Is this yours?"

Miss Dunham nodded. "We can talk inside."

She picked her way towards the motorhome across open ground, weaving around a series of booby traps that I guessed she had laid herself. They included tripwires attached to tin cans, and a freshly dug pit covered with branches and leaves. I followed in her footsteps, taking care not to trigger any of the traps. We paused on a set of foldaway steps beneath a red-and-white-striped awning that extended from the vehicle's roofline. She explained that it added extra cover from satellite surveillance, though not the ones with infrared detection. As she fiddled with the lock, the sound of the third most popular Billy Dark tribute act in the south-west drifted over the resort.

The door opened with a click. "In you go," barked Miss Dunham. "That awning won't fool those military satellites for long."

I jumped at the command. Something about a teacher's voice, especially a gym teacher, had a deep and immediate effect. Her voice was even more commanding than the Alien Overlord's, and I was beginning to suspect that this might be the real Miss Dunham after all.

No sooner had I entered than she grabbed me by the

arm and prised off the purple rubber wristband I'd been given when I arrived at Great Minds. She marched to a tiny galley kitchen, opened a microwave and tossed it inside. Before I realised what she was doing, she had set the machine to cook on High. There were sparks from the circuit board embedded in the rubber, then the whole thing began to smoke. After a minute she removed what remained of the wristband. Charred and melted, it was beyond repair.

"Tracking device," said Miss Dunham. "Can't be too careful."

I recoiled at the acrid smell of burnt rubber. I remained unconvinced that it was any sort of tracker. All I knew was that I'd just lost my free food cart privileges.

"I know what you're thinking," she said, closing a pair of heavy brown curtains across the vehicle's windows. "That I am not who I say I am." With a curt gesture she invited me to take a seat at the swing-out table for two in light oak. "This will put your mind at rest." She handed me an iPad set up to play a video. It showed Miss Dunham sitting in some sort of hospital room next to a large piece of medical equipment. She spoke directly to the camera.

"To whomever is watching this, the following will prove beyond reasonable doubt that I am the real Susan

Dunham and not one of those disgusting alien creatures wearing me like a human tracksuit."

For the next few minutes I watched as the Miss Dunham on screen underwent a series of tests, culminating in some sort of live scan that showed a picture of her insides. The Alien Overlord had hidden tentacles – the woman in the video was full of intestines and other squishy bits, but she was clearly no alien.

"I agree that she is definitely human," I said. "But how do I know that's *you*? Unless you carry out the same tests in front of me, I can't possibly be certain."

She banged a fist on the table. "You're right. Why didn't I think of that?" She leapt up from her chair and began to perform pull-ups on a metal bar set across the width of the cramped interior. "Maybe I could get hold of the test equipment, bring it here, but no – you can't run a full-body scanner off a 12-volt car battery."

I had an idea. She wasn't the only one who'd had her body hijacked recently. "They took Miss Dunham's body, but not her mind. So perhaps there's something in your and Zack's – I mean, *our* – shared past that only the real Susan Dunham would know."

With a grunt she did one last pull-up and then dropped to the floor. "Smart thinking, Zack. But don't call me Susan. I may not be your teacher any more, but

there are lines we do not cross."

The more time I spent with her the more I considered that she almost certainly was my former teacher. She sat back down at the table and fixed me with a grave expression.

"I have two words for you." She held up a finger with each one. "Crystal. Palace."

I had no idea what she was talking about, but I think she took my silence for something other than ignorance.

"I know we promised never to speak of this again, but under the circumstances I have no option. I hope you can forgive me."

I realised she was waiting for my consent. "Uh, yeah. Under the circumstances, sure."

She looked past me, her eyes fixed on some hazy point in the distance. "It was the day of the south-east inter-schools swimming gala at the Crystal Palace National Sports Centre. You were odds-on favourite for the hundred-metre backstroke – not that I laid an each-way bet on you, as that would have been unethical. You emerged from the changing room and were about to take your place poolside in front of a packed audience, when I whipped a towel around you. I had noticed that your Speedos were, how shall I put it, holed beneath the waterline. Thankfully, I was quickly able to obtain a replacement pair from Lost Property and you went on to win the competition."

That explained why all the photos from the day showed Zack in a pair of Finding Nemo trunks. Well, that was one mystery solved.

"If it hadn't been for me, Zack, you would have been horribly exposed in front of your peers." Miss Dunham shook her head slowly. "No worse fate could befall a teenage boy. You swore me to silence and I have honoured our pinkie swear from that day to this."

I was convinced. "Miss Dunham," I said. "It is you."

"And, Zack Parker, it is you…" Her mouth became a thin line. "…who is Star Lad."

I laughed off her suggestion. "I don't know what you're talking about. I'm just Zack Parker, an ordinary, if rather annoying, schoolboy."

Miss Dunham wasn't to be dissuaded so easily. She dropped to the floor, lay on her back with her knees drawn up and began to do crunches.

"Remember, I was there in the gym with that alien *thing* pretending to be me. It tied me up. I saw your little brother, Lance—"

Really? "Luke. He's called Luke."

"OK, whatever. I saw Luke and—"

"I mean, he was in your class for a whole term and you

can't remember his name?"

"Hey, I'm a gym teacher, not Marvin the Memory Man."

She flipped on to her front and commenced doing squat thrusts. The motorhome rocked with the force of her exercising, its suspension squeaking under her powerful, thigh-burning moves.

"After what I witnessed that day, my eyes were opened. I saw that I had been living a lie. They feed us lies, Zack, to stop us from probing. To make us think that we're safe, that life is normal – just one long round of stacking crash mats, resisting the staff room biscuit tin, taking dodgeballs to the noggin'. But real life is far from normal." She got to her feet and gazed out of the window. "The truth is out there – and it's wearing tentacles." She turned to me, not even a little breathless from her exertions. "The day after I saw the alien in the gym I went straight down to WH Smith, cancelled my *Muscle & Fitness* magazine subscription and took out one for *UFO Quarterly*. I joined some online forums frequented by like-minded souls, people who not only believed my story but had even wilder stories of their own." She adjusted her towelling headband. I glimpsed a shiny lining – it appeared to be made of tinfoil. "I went to conventions: Con-Spiracy, Decepti-Con, Congleton.

Yeah, that one was a mistake." She swung up a finger. "And I followed your little brother."

"You did what?!"

"It was the question that tantalised me most of all – what could the alien have wanted with him? What made him so special? At first I wondered if *he* might be Star Lad, and that his pathetic performance in the gym had merely been a clever distraction. But no, it turned out that he is genuinely hopeless."

"That's a bit harsh," I protested, but she wasn't listening.

"Finally, I tracked him to his base of operations. A humble tree house. I used my gym-teacher skills to climb on to the roof. And I waited. I waited in the rain. In the cold. I didn't care. I clung to that roof and listened in on his conversations. I heard *everything*. I know all about S.C.A.R.F. I know that Serge eats way too much sugar. I know about Dark Flutter. I know about *you*."

I attempted to deny it but there was little point. She had all the facts on her side. Well, almost. Although she claimed to know everything, there was one detail that had escaped her. She didn't suspect that I was Luke in Zack's body. I wasn't sure how much I could trust her, so I decided to keep that to myself for now.

"After six nights on the tree-house roof I sold

everything I owned, bought this motorhome and I've been on the road ever since. Honing my already impressive body. Acquiring new mental strength." She gestured to a shelf with a neatly arranged stack of Nintendo brain-training games. "And now I am ready."

"For what, exactly?"

She pulled a binder from the same shelf. It was filled with photographs. She removed one and slammed it down on the table between us.

"McMinville, Oregon, 1950."

It was a black-and-white photograph showing a corner of a house and, in the sky above, a small black disc. She placed down the next photograph.

"Drakensberg Mountains, South Africa, 1956."

Another black-and-white shot. This one taken among the clouds, looking down on a silver saucer-shaped aircraft. Suddenly I understood what I was looking at.

They were photos of UFOs.

Miss Dunham continued her slideshow, producing a succession of out-of-focus pictures of circular, triangular and cigar-shaped objects. She rattled off the details of each sighting.

"Waikiki, Hawaii, 1959. Costa Rica, 1971. Gulf Breeze, Florida, 1987. Bromley, 2016."

When she'd finished there was an impressive stack

of photographs between us. She lowered her voice to a whisper. "Zack, this is no ordinary leisure resort with insufficient staffing and questionable health and safety procedures." Her eyes swivelled left and right, checking for imaginary eavesdroppers. "It's a UFO landing site." With a click of metal rings she removed one last photograph from her binder and added it to the pile.

"They're preparing for *another* invasion." She smiled thinly. "But those aliens are in for a nasty surprise, now that you're here."

I was about to ask her why my presence made a difference, and then I remembered that, of course, she believed I was Star Lad. Uh-oh. I couldn't go up against an alien invasion force, not in my current powerless condition. If Miss Dunham was relying on me to save the world, then six billion human beings were in deep trouble.

7
THE BLURRY SIGHTING

"She's crazy," said Zack. "Miss Dunham has quite obviously vaulted off her rocker."

It was the following morning and I had gathered the members of S.C.A.R.F. together in a booth in Eggheads, the resort's breakfast diner. Mum and Dad had joined us briefly, but the lure of the spa was too great and they'd headed off after a swift bowl of cornflakes and a waffle. They said they would just dip in and then join us later for a bike ride. Unfortunately, it seemed they were serious about spending some quality family time together. In the meantime I had other things to worry about. Following Miss Dunham's revelation about the true nature of Great Minds I had returned to my berth to endure a fitful night's sleep. I'd tossed and turned, her words keeping me awake and then, when I finally dropped off, invading my dreams.

"Does she have any proof?" asked Lara.

I made space on the table and set down the very last photograph she had shown me, which she'd reluctantly passed over, but only after making me sign a disclaimer agreeing not to divulge the contents of our conversation to anyone other than members of S.C.A.R.F. until the year 2049.

"And what is that meant to be?" asked Zack.

The photograph was out of focus and the details indistinct. When she had presented it to me last night I had struggled to figure out what it showed. I didn't expect the others to fare any better.

Serge tapped a finger lightly on the image. "It is evident that here is a photograph of an Unidentified Flying Object hovering above what is quite clearly the boating lake at the centre of the park."

The others leaned in, squinting to see what he had so easily recognised.

"It was taken twelve years ago, two years before the park was built," I explained. "There are lots of people who believe it's a genuine flying saucer. UFO fans have

even given it a name. The Blurry Sighting."

"No wonder," said Lara. "I can't make out a thing."

"Not that kind of 'blurry'. The land that the resort occupies used to be a Saxon village called Greater Blurreigh."

Zack gave a dismissive sigh. "Oh, come on, Luke. Tell me you're not so desperate to act out your superhero fantasies that you believe any of this? Don't you see what's really going on? Miss Dunham was traumatised by what happened to her in the gym and now she imagines aliens are everywhere. She lives in a motorhome. She probably wears a tinfoil hat to protect her from mind-control."

Actually, it was a tinfoil towelling headband. But yeah.

"She's become a conspiracy nut," he said through a mouthful of fruit.

He'd ordered the fresh fruit bowl for breakfast. No chocolate sprinkles, no marshmallow pieces – *what* was he doing to my body?

"You mustn't encourage her, it's not fair. The poor woman needs help." Zack pushed away his bowl. "Now, I have something of *real* importance to discuss with you." He glanced at the other two. "Alone."

Lara and Serge took the hint and slipped out of the booth. Hand-in-hand they strolled off to investigate the more interesting end of the breakfast buffet. Whatever

Zack had to tell me must be highly sensitive if he couldn't talk about it in front of them.

"You're keeping that date with Cara," he said.

It took me a moment to figure out what he was on about. "Oh, you mean the yoga thing."

"That counts. She's never asked me to go anywhere with her, until now."

"Technically, she asked me, not you."

"You are me, in case you'd forgotten."

I didn't know anything about this boy-girl stuff, but I remembered something Mum had once said. "Maybe it's my personality she likes."

Zack let out a half-gasp, half-laugh. "Uh, no, it's not. Trust me on that one." He gazed at me unblinkingly. "This is my chance to get close to her. Unfortunately, that means you have to steer the ship until I get back into my own body. Luke, don't mess this up for me."

Zack had kissed an evil cyborg Cara and an identical version of her from another dimension, but what he wanted most of all was to be *this* Cara's boyfriend. Now, in a horrifying twist, it seemed that responsibility had fallen on me.

"So here's what you do. First, you have to stop talking to her about dorky stuff like role-playing games and comics. It's off-putting in the romantic arena."

I wanted to hear more about this arena – was it like the Coliseum with gladiators and lions and hideous deaths?

"Say little, listen to her when she talks, and if she asks anything you don't know the answer to, just nod and distract her with a question of your own."

"Like, which Green Lantern became Parallax?"

I watched as his lower lip trembled with anger.

"I'm kidding," I said. He couldn't take a joke, not even in my body.

"Fine. Whatever. And don't think you can duck out of the date," he said. "I'll be checking up on you."

Our conversation was cut short by a series of musical "bings" and "bongs". It was the sound of the resort's public address system, and it meant that an announcement was incoming.

"Good morning, Great Minds!" boomed a cheery voice.

When you heard the announcer's greeting, you were supposed to reply with the park slogan: "You Think You're So Clever!"

The diner rang with the phrase as everyone shouted it out, even Zack. But not me. I was not one of life's joiners-in. The only things I belonged to were S.C.A.R.F. and the library.

The announcement continued. "Will participants in

the 5k Head-Scratcher Fun Run please come to the start line. On your marks, get set, go, go, go!"

"What's a Head-Scratcher Fun Run?" I asked.

"It's a cross-country run where every two hundred metres you have to solve an increasingly difficult algebra equation."

My mind boggled. "Who would choose to do something like that on holiday – or, indeed, ever?"

"Right, I'm off," said Zack, taking one last mouthful of fruit. "I've heard there are six hundred metres on factorising quadratic expressions," he added excitedly.

What a surprise – my brother had signed up for the swottiest five-kilometre run in history. Well, if he thought that my legs were going to carry him round a course that length, he was in for an unpleasant surprise.

I sat alone at the table toying with my egg-white omelette. Zack had vetoed what he called non-nutritional breakfast items, which meant I ended up with this glistening, maggot-white dish. I pushed it away with my fork and glanced over at Serge, who was piling a plate at the buffet. I attempted to use my telepathic power to communicate with him. Closing my eyes, I focused on two key words. "Chocolate muffin, chocolate muffin, chocolate muffin..."

When I opened them again, Lara and Serge had

returned to the booth.

"You look like you could do with one of these," he said, setting down a double-chocolate muffin.

I almost fell out of my chair. "It worked!"

"What are you talking about?"

I wasn't yet ready to confess to them my difficulties with Zack's powers. But perhaps the moment was not far off. On the one hand, this was a minor triumph; on the other, I probably couldn't save the world using only the power of muffin-summoning. Also, given Serge's fondness for them, there was a very good chance that my telepathy had failed and that he had chosen it without any influence from me.

I took a big bite and my thoughts turned to Miss Dunham. I didn't feel the same way about her as Zack. What she'd said to me last night was just the kind of outrageous claim I'd typically come up with – and no one ever believed me at first, either. Or, was he on to something when he called her a conspiracy nut?

"Zack was right," I said, putting down the muffin. "Miss Dunham does need help." I looked round at the others. "Our help."

Serge poked his nose in the air and sniffed. "Patchouli and lavender and *what*?"

True, it was not the response I'd expected, but

his outburst became clear a moment later when our dedicated host, Sarah Pelham, rocked up to the booth.

"Hello, Brain-boxes," she greeted us in her usual annoying fashion.

"Hello, Sarah," we all chimed in a half-hearted response.

"Let me tell you about a host of super-fun activities on here today at Great Minds." She extended both index fingers and pointed them at us like a couple of six-shooters, narrowed one eye and said, "Just for super-smart children like *you*."

"Do you *have* to tell us?" I asked.

She looked puzzled and a little disheartened by my response, but sadly it didn't last.

"Hey, Zack," she addressed me. "I just saw your little brother lining up for the Head-Scratcher Fun Run. How about you? Got to keep active." She tapped my head like she was knocking on a door. "A stimulated brain is a happy brain."

I rubbed the now tender area of my skull.

"He does not do running," explained Serge with an apologetic air. "At least, not voluntarily."

"Fun Run," Sarah repeated, for no obvious reason.

"Yes, we heard you," I said, growing irritated at her persistence. I had decided to go and see Miss Dunham,

and Sarah was delaying me.

"Fun. Run." She said it again, this time emphasising each word.

"Are you OK?" asked Lara.

I glanced up. Sarah's mouth twitched, her eyes stared blankly towards the breakfast buffet. Her permanently cheery expression slipped. "Fun," she said in a cold voice.

Frightened eyes found us.

"RUN!"

We sat there, unsure how to react. Was she strongly encouraging us to take part in the Fun Run? Was she on a commission? Or was it something else? But as quickly as these questions arose, her face resumed its previous happily bland expression. She grinned, turned on her heel and strolled off, but not before giving us a wave and one final cheery exclamation.

"Have a mind-blowing day!"

8
THE WARM-UP MISSION

The Smug-Buggy trundled off into the distance, winding back towards the main resort. We waited until it had disappeared around a bend in the road and set off the rest of the way on foot. Our destination lay at the far edge of the resort, beyond the limits of the self-driving vehicles.

"OK, you have to admit, that was weird," said Lara.

She was referring to the business with Sarah Pelham in the diner. We hadn't discussed it during the journey, because we were wary of the buggy's monitoring capabilities. In comics and films you can never trust autonomous machines.

"Did you see her face?" said Serge. "She seemed scared."

"I think she'd just caught sight of my omelette."

"There's another explanation," said Lara. "The pressure to be that chirpy all the time would get to anyone. Maybe she just cracked."

I resisted making another omelette joke. We agreed to keep an eye on Sarah, but her one-time odd behaviour didn't justify raising the threat level from salmon. We headed into the long grass and a short time later reached the clearing where Miss Dunham had parked her motorhome.

"Watch out for the trip—" I hissed, but it was too late. Serge stumbled into the ankle-high string stretched across the perimeter of the clearing where Miss Dunham's motorhome was parked. A collection of empty tin cans tied to the end of the string clashed together, setting off the alarm. A moment later the door flew open revealing Miss Dunham crouched in the doorway clutching what looked like a trombone, which she proceeded to sweep back and forth. I raised a hand and mouthed an apology.

"What are they doing here?" She indicated Serge and Lara.

"Reinforcements," I said. If there was any truth to Miss Dunham's alien suspicions, I needed all the help

I could get.

Miss Dunham nodded curtly, kicked out the fold-down steps and motioned us inside.

As we climbed in, she pointed the trombone appliance at each of us in turn. "Argon detector – picks up scatter-debris from alien spacecraft engines," she explained while shoving it in Serge's face.

"Um, isn't argon a gas found in Earth's atmosphere?" said Lara. "Like found *a lot*."

Miss Dunham tapped the side of her head with a finger. "That's how cunning these aliens are." She took a reading from the trombone, checked a display and announced, "Clear." She shoved Lara inside. "Next."

Once all of us had been cleared (of *what*, I had no clue), Miss Dunham insisted that Lara and Serge surrender their resort wristbands. As she'd done with mine, she flung them in the microwave and, over Serge's wails, blasted them to pieces. Only after that did the meeting begin. Lara and Serge sat down at the swing-out table for two, which meant there wasn't room for me.

"Don't just stand there, give me twenty pull-ups," ordered Miss Dunham.

"Is this really necessary?" I objected. "Shouldn't we be concentrating on the invasion?"

"What do you think this is? We're preparing. We

have to be in peak physical shape for what's coming." She stared at Lara and Serge. "Don't know what you're smirking about – you two are next."

Their smiles vanished faster than a four-fingered KitKat that has strayed within Serge's reach. Miss Dunham grabbed the whistle hanging around her neck, popped it between her lips and gave a sharp blow. "BEGIN!"

Reluctantly, I gripped the metal bar, took a deep breath and pulled. To my immense surprise I felt my arm muscles flex and my body rise up. My chin met the bar for the first time in my life. I did it again. This was easy in Zack's body. Of course it was – everything was easier as Zack.

Miss Dunham looked around the interior of the motorhome. "Hold on a minute..."

At what I took to be her command, I froze mid-pull.

"Where's Larry?"

"Who?"

"That little brother of yours. From what I can remember of my time on the roof of the tree house, I got the vivid impression that he was up to his skinny elbows in this S.C.A.R.F. business."

Exhaling, I lowered myself to the floor. "*Luke* is out of the picture, for now," I said pointedly.

Miss Dunham narrowed her eyes. "Why? What's happened to him?"

Uh-oh, I could tell she was about to go off on another paranoid rant.

"Has his body been taken over by an alien presence?" she asked. "Is he under some kind of evil mind-control?"

Actually, she wasn't far off the mark with that one.

Miss Dunham took my silence as confirmation of her suspicion. She slapped a fist into her open palm. "I knew it!"

Lara glared at me. I think she was irritated that I'd accidentally encouraged one of Miss Dunham's nutty fantasies. She turned sweetly to the gym teacher and raised her hand as if she was in class.

"Miss, why do you think there's going to be an alien invasion now? Great Minds has been here for years."

Her attempt to change the subject worked. Miss Dunham grabbed a map of the resort from her shelf and rolled it out on the table.

"This is why," she said, prodding a finger at a dome-shaped building that squatted next to the boating pond. It differed from the other domes scattered throughout the park. This one was wider and flatter. I was going to say saucer-shaped, but I felt that would only send Miss Dunham into another fantastical rant. Also, it was

helpfully labelled.

"Brainwaves?"

"It's an indoor water park, construction of which only finished in the last few weeks. However, I believe that it is no innocent brain-themed swimming attraction, but a command-and-control base. From here the aliens on the ground will coordinate the attack from above."

"So you think they are already present on Earth?" said Serge.

"I think an advance party has been here for a very long time." She waved a hand over the map. "This place has been a hotspot of UFO activity since the Blurreigh Sighting."

I wanted so much to believe her, but I could see the doubt in my friends' eyes.

"I have fresh evidence," she continued, angling the laptop so that we could all see the screen. "I recorded this during my latest surveillance sweep."

She prodded a key and a video began to play. It looked like it had been filmed from deep in the undergrowth. Leaves and scrub trailed over the lens, which was pointed at the entrance to Brainwaves. Miss Dunham's voice punctuated scenes of not very exciting activity.

"Zero nine hundred hours. Family of four enter the water park. No alien activity." There was a jump cut and the time code leapt forward an hour. Now, along with her narration, there was a distinct crunching noise on the soundtrack. "Ten hundred hours. Possible spike in argon reading, although that may be due to my carrot sticks. Still no sign of alien activity. In fact, *suspiciously low level of alien activity*." The video moved on again. "Wait! Irregular movement in quadrant two." The camera jerked to one side, focusing in on a brown-and-white cat sitting quietly next to a bush, licking itself.

"It's a cat video," Lara whispered. "She's showing us cat videos."

Miss Dunham overheard. "Not the cat. *There*."

In the background of the shot was a white van with writing on the side. The camera moved again and it came into focus. "E.T. Electricals," I read. Surely she didn't think…

Miss Dunham paused the video. "There, what did I tell you! Tell me that's not a sign of an alien conspiracy?"

I could see that Lara was about to tell her exactly that, so I got in first.

"Well, that's settled then," I said.

"What is?" asked Lara.

"We need to get inside that command-and-control dome."

"Just what I was thinking," agreed Miss Dunham.

"Infiltrate and expose them." She hustled Lara out of her chair and sat down in front of the map. "Now, we have to assume that we'll be walking into a trap."

It was difficult to tell what her conclusion was based on, since her paranoia was operating at a level that meant to her everything appeared to be a trap. Discarded crisp packet? *Trap*. Unreliable resort signage? *Trap*. Suspiciously empty park bench? *Death-trap*.

Lara pulled me to one side, out of earshot of our gym teacher. "What are you playing at? You don't actually believe her?"

"Look at it like this," I said. "We go in and either we find an alien air-traffic controller plotting the downfall of the human race." I shrugged. "Or changing rooms."

"Or it could be—" began Serge, but Lara cut him off.

"One word about an evil blancmange, and minigolf is off."

He held up his hands in surrender.

"OK, team," said Miss Dunham. "Devising a plan to break into a hostile alien command-and-control base can't be any harder than coming up with a lesson plan for you lot. And since time is of the essence, we'll make our move as soon as I've finalised the details." She pulled out an old-fashioned stopwatch and clicked the button. The hands began to sweep around the face. "I'll meet you at the dome in one hour."

"I can't," I said. "I have yoga."

Miss Dunham frowned at me. In the quiet of the motorhome the only sound was the tick of the stopwatch. I think she was waiting for me to explain, but there was no way I could tell her the truth. I decided to play into her paranoia. "It'll look suspicious if I don't keep my appointment. We don't want to alert Them to our plan."

"Good thinking, Zack," said Miss Dunham. "Also, you'll be nicely warmed up for the infiltration. Fine. After your yoga session then." She glared at us. "What are you all standing there for? Scatter!" With that, she gave another blast on her whistle and we scrambled for the door.

Perhaps Lara was right and the dome held nothing more unusual than the Cortex Café and the Spinal Cord Splash Pad. But if not, then I'd finally get to put my superpowers to the test. I just hoped they'd be there when I needed them.

9
CONTROL-CENTRE-PARK

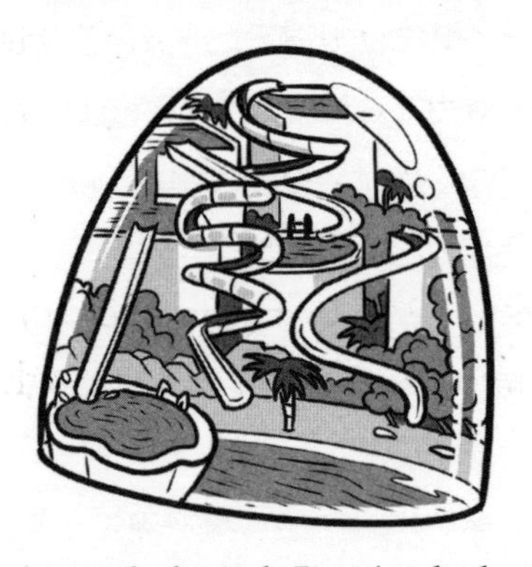

The yoga class ended and I exited the Mindfulness Centre. An hour of downward-facing dog and assorted poses had not triggered a body swap, although I did feel surprisingly relaxed. I wondered if all that stretching had loosened me up enough to access Zack's superpowers. Maybe a quick flight across the park? I glanced around. No one was watching.

"Up, up and away," I muttered. "Blast-off! Launch! Go! Fly, my pretties! Oh, for—"

"What are you doing?"

It was my brother, red-faced, hair plastered to his head after the ill-advised Fun Run, sucking down a

Great Guzzler drink through a bendy straw.

"Nothing," I lied.

He steered me across the square, which for some reason was called a *piazza* (that's Italian for town square, but strangely not the word for a square pizza).

"How was it? What did Cara say?" He took another gulp of his oversized drink. "Tell me everything."

"Uh, there's not much to report."

"She must have said something."

"Let me think. Oh yes. You're not very flexible."

Zack was mildly offended. "I thought I was quite supple."

I shrugged.

There was a gurgle and a slurp as he reached the bottom of the Great Guzzler. I was surprised that Zack would put something so unhealthy into his body. It was the sort of drink that I'd choose, not him. He picked up on my unspoken judgement.

"It's a smoothie in disguise," he said. "Kale, cabbage and soy milk."

Even the list of ingredients made me feel ill. We carried on walking while I fielded a string of questions about Cara.

"I really have to go now," I told Zack. I was concerned about keeping Miss Dunham waiting. I didn't think

she was allowed to give me detention but I couldn't be entirely confident.

"Wait," said Zack. "Did you notice any of the signs?"

He hadn't told me to keep an eye out for that sort of thing. "You mean like ancient runes?"

He sighed. "I mean body language. Did Cara smile at you, run a hand through her hair, throw back her head and give a tinkly laugh, touch your arm, turn her body towards you like this, or like this?" He adopted a series of what looked to me like highly uncomfortable poses. It was all very confusing, but before I could comment he grabbed my arm. "You didn't say anything dorky, did you? Because I warned you about—"

I brushed off his concern. "Relax, you were awesome. Cool, composed, funny."

"Funny?" He sounded even more concerned. "Tell me you didn't try one of your stupid jokes on her."

Um. Yeah. "What do you take me for?" I blustered.

He let it slide, keen to find out more. "So am I seeing her again? How did you leave it?"

That was the odd part. Even though Cara hadn't laughed at the one about the second-level Wizard and the Gelatinous Cube, when the class finished she'd flicked me with her towel (ouch) and said we should do this again. It didn't seem much to me, but when I informed

Zack he clenched his fists and did a little hopping dance, closing his eyes and saying "thank you" over and over.

Just then, Cara herself sauntered out of the Mindfulness Centre, ponytail swinging, gym-bag slung over one shoulder. She walked past us without comment, but then glanced back at me.

"I'll be at Brainwaves later this afternoon."

I wasn't sure why she was informing me of her schedule.

"Maybe see you there," she added.

Beside me, my brother let out an excited squeak.

"Sorry," I said. "I'm bus— Oww!"

Zack-as-me had stepped on my foot.

"He'll be there," he said firmly.

With a puzzled shake of her head, Cara went on her way.

"Amazing!" said my brother, when she was out of earshot. "*She* wants *me* to hang out with her."

Technically, she'd asked me-as-Zack to hang out with her, but I didn't point that out to my brother, since he would have launched into a big discussion and I'd just spotted Lara on the other side of the piazza. She waved at me from the cab of the Smug-Buggy. Time to go. I left my overexcited sibling and joined her and Serge. Tossing my Deadpool backpack in first, I jumped into my seat.

"All right, let's get this over with," said Lara with a sigh. "Take us to Brainwaves," she instructed the Smug-Buggy. With a silent surge of power, the Highly Autonomous Land-vehicle complied, and we were off.

As we sped through the resort, I reflected on the upcoming mission. With a bit of luck it would result in an exciting battle with alien commandos, and people pointing to the sky in wonder as I flew past. However, I could tell that Serge and Lara remained highly doubtful. And if I was honest, even I had some practical objections. For example, I didn't know if alien invaders kept a joint diary, or called each other first to avoid accidentally turning up to invade the same planet at the same time, but we'd only just fought off one invasion. The chances of another following hot on its heels were slim.

"We have arrived," announced Serge five minutes later, as the Smug Buggy pulled up outside our destination.

Brainwaves lay before us, a wonky glass dome containing a collection of fake beaches and overheated swimming pools linked together by a series of water slides. As far as Miss Dunham's plan to infiltrate her imagined command-and-control base went, the first part was a doddle. We were guests, which meant we didn't have to break in using a grappling hook and highly convincing masks of lifeguards' faces. Instead, we simply strolled through the front door.

The hot, sticky air inside the dome was filled with the mingled aroma of chips from the Cortex Café and coffee from the Hypothalamespresso Bar. We stood on the edge of the main pool area. Two giant speakers suspended from the ceiling blasted out a repetitive tune that competed with the shouts of children splashing about and ignoring the "no diving" sign. I picked out Josh among them. He was using a large beach ball as a weapon. I think he was trying to drown Adrian Marsh from Year 8 but I couldn't be sure. There was a wave machine, but instead of a surge of towering surf all it produced was an apologetic dribble. Like every other attraction at Great Minds, this one was badly maintained and a potential hazard. Even the fire alarm had an out-of-order sign posted on it.

Lara cast her eye around the place. "Doesn't look much like an alien command-and-control base."

"We said we'd help her," I reminded her. "What's the worst that can happen?"

To answer that I only had to glance at Josh, who was now definitely trying to drown Adrian.

We put the first part of the plan into action. To maintain the deception that we were normal guests we hit the changing rooms. I pulled my swimming trunks

out of the backpack, taking care not to reveal Zack's Star Lad costume, which I had stuffed inside. I noticed that there was something stuck to the cape. It looked like an old chewy sweet. He was not going to be pleased.

We re-emerged a short time later to gather by the side of the main pool.

"Nice trunks," said Lara, admiring Serge's Aquaman-themed pair.

They were nice, especially compared with the plain blue pair of Zack's I was forced to wear.

"*Merci*, Lara," he replied. "They are the limited edition."

"You surprise me," she said.

A whistle shrilled across Brainwaves. It belonged to one of the patrolling lifeguards.

"You three, no running in the pool area!"

"But we're not running," Lara objected. She hated to be told off. Being reprimanded came quite naturally to me so I didn't give it a second thought.

The lifeguard approached. Like the rest of her colleagues she carried a foam swimming float and wore a water-blue costume stamped with the Great Minds logo, flip-flops and a grey swimming cap. Her goggles were pulled down over her face, and as she padded closer she pulled up one eye-cup and whispered, "It's me."

To no one's great surprise it was indeed Miss Dunham, in disguise.

"Right, you lot, we need to go through my plan without drawing unnecessary attention to ourselves."

"We could assemble in the Hypothalamespresso Bar," suggested Serge. "I observed some tempting *biscotti*."

Miss Dunham ignored him and pointed. "All of you, in the pool."

We lowered ourselves into the water and, at her command, began to swim up and down the length of the pool. Miss Dunham trotted alongside, interspersing details of her plan with a lengthy criticism of Serge's crawl technique.

"I pulled the resort blueprints off Plans Within Plans. It's an online conspiracy resource." She turned around the foam swimming float. Stuck to the back of it was a layout of Brainwaves. "It's laminated."

She'd thought of everything.

"See here," she said. "There's a hidden underground complex beneath Brainwaves that isn't on the official plans."

The layout was marked with symbols, none of which were alien. It looked to me like a boring collection of stairways, locker rooms and a toilet. I remembered reading that beneath Disney World lay a massive

network of tunnels, a hidden city, used by the staff to get around the park unseen by guests. I assumed this was Great Minds' greatly reduced version. Nothing more mysterious than that. As for the goal of our mission, Miss Dunham's command-and-control centre, it appeared to be a large, circular room slap-bang in the middle, labelled "Store".

"What about this lift next to the café?" I asked, indicating one of the symbols. "It looks like it goes directly to the room you're talking about."

Serge snapped his fingers. "Miss Dunham, what if you pretended to be room service and we all hid under the food trolley? They would suspect *nothing*, and we could pick up some delicious snacks at the same time."

"Do aliens order room service?" asked Lara.

"Those from advanced civilisations, *oui*."

"Even if that wasn't a ridiculous idea," said Miss Dunham, "the lift is secured by some kind of strange lock."

"What do you mean, strange?" I asked.

"I recced it earlier. Couldn't get in no matter what I tried. There's no key, no keypad, no facial-recognition camera. Then, just as I was leaving, I saw that Sarah Pelham person. Actually, I didn't see her so much as smell her. That perfume! She strolled past me, straight into the lift. The doors opened like magic for her. But that doesn't help us."

I reached the far end of the pool and kicked off for the return leg, a clear two metres ahead of Lara and Serge. As in everything else, my brother was an excellent swimmer.

Miss Dunham returned her attention to the plans. "I think our best option is this inspection hatch midway along the water slide."

The three of us swam to the edge for a better look.

"See here, in the Cerebral Aqueduct." She traced a finger along its length. "At exactly twenty-two metres. Looks like it's used to access the water slide from the dry side, but we could go in the opposite direction. The hatch opens into the tunnel network. Then we make our way to this point." She tapped the plan. "It's an emergency exit for the command-and-control centre. They'll never see us coming."

Lara studied the plans and voiced her first concern. "Based on the distance and the drop, by the time we reach the first hatch I estimate that we'll be travelling along the Cerebral Aqueduct at thirty kilometres an hour. For your plan to work we'll have to find some way of rapidly slowing to a stop."

Miss Dunham turned to me with a knowing look.

"Zack, that's your department."

"Well, we could wear suction cups on our hands and feet, or attach ourselves to a bungee cord, or—"

Miss Dunham gave me a puzzled look. "Or you could use your force-field power to create a block in the tunnel?"

Uh-oh. I hadn't yet managed to get Zack's powers online and now the mission hinged on using them. This could be problematic.

Lara pointed out another potential flaw in the plan. "The Cerebral Aqueduct is the most popular water slide in Brainwaves. It's in constant use, so what do we do about the other kids?"

Miss Dunham considered the question. "Think of it like a netball match, when one player has to sacrifice herself to allow her teammates to score."

It was fair to say that Miss Dunham taught an unorthodox style of netball.

"You mean a diversion," I said.

"I volunteer," Serge said quickly. "I will pretend to be frozen in fear at the top of the slide, thus impeding the progress of the children lining up behind me."

He sent an uneasy glance in my direction. Serge wasn't a fan of water slides or rollercoasters or anything that made his stomach turn somersaults, and this way he would have a perfect excuse not to descend the nerve-shattering ride. I had a feeling he wouldn't need to fake his anxiety.

"It's going to take time to get the hatch open," said Miss Dunham. "Can you make enough fuss to give us thirty seconds?"

"It will be *difficile*, but I shall simulate sheer terror."

Lara squeezed his arm and smiled. "You're so resourceful."

"OK then, we're all set." Miss Dunham adjusted her swimming cap and I saw something under it glint in the artificial light. It looked like a tinfoil lining. She wasn't taking any chances with alien mind-control.

I placed my palms on the tiled floor and began to haul myself out of the pool.

"What are you doing?" She pressed a damp flip-flop on my outspread fingers. "Get back in there. I want five more lengths, for appearance's sake."

Once a gym teacher, always a gym teacher. As we swam, I should have confessed to Lara and Serge that I couldn't generate a force field. But I was too embarrassed.

The three of us completed the extra lengths and joined the queue for the Cerebral Aqueduct. As Lara had predicted, an impatient line of children waited to launch themselves down the corkscrewing slide. The

queue shrank as each one pushed off with a yell of fearful excitement and soon I was near the top. It was my task to go down first, stopping at the twenty-two-metre mark next to the inspection hatch. As the others followed I would use my force field to stop them too. I realised that this was my last chance to tell the others I couldn't do it, and I was just about to confess when there was a commotion behind me. Someone was trying to force his way to the front of the queue. With a sinking feeling I saw that it was Josh Khan, clutching the beach ball I'd seen him with earlier. He recognised the members of S.C.A.R.F. and regarded us with deep and familiar suspicion.

"What are you lot up to now?"

"AAAAH!" Serge swooned, teetering on the edge of the slide. "I have faltered on the brink! Is this a giant dessert I see before me? I cannot go on! The terror, she has gripped me. *J'ai peur!*" He clutched his throat with both hands. "The fear, the fear!"

Josh and the rest of the queue were distracted by Serge's memorable, if rather overwrought, performance. As was I, until Miss Dunham hissed in my ear.

"Zack, go!"

I stepped to the precipice. There was no turning back now.

10
BOUNCING BOY!

I was poised on the edge of disaster. Never mind Star Lad, I wasn't even a third-rate superhero like Arm Fall-Off Boy, or Stone Boy, or Bouncing Boy.

Wait a minute!

I had an idea. Grabbing the beach ball out of Josh's hands, I stepped off. His shout of objection faded as I plummeted down the slide. The initial, near-vertical drop accelerated me to warp speed and in seconds I was slipping down the Cerebral Aqueduct like a photon torpedo in trunks. My idea was simple, but risky. Bouncing Boy was one of the worst superheroes ever created, his only power the ability to blow himself up

like a beach ball. Taking a bend too fast, I shot out of the channel and sailed into the air, almost losing my grip on the precious ball. A second later I landed heavily, my bottom skidding along the base of the flume, my legs stretched out before me creating a bow wave. I searched the smooth surface of the ball until I located the nub of a valve, pulled it out with my teeth and began to blow furiously. With a whoosh I entered the tunnel section of the water slide, swiftly passing the ten-metre mark. My feverish puffs inflated the ball way beyond its safe limits, but I had to take the risk. Fifteen metres. I corrected my approach for the final stretch. I could see the outline of the hatch at twenty-two metres and could feel the beach ball stretched explosively taut in my hands.

I slapped the valve shut and jammed the ball against the roof of the slide. It acted like a plug, the force of friction causing me to slow down. The ball complained at its treatment in a high-pitched squeak. I held my breath, with every passing second expecting it to pop, but it held its shape, dragging against the roof to bring me to a controlled stop just a metre or two beyond the hatch. Relief washed over me like a wave from a properly maintained wave machine. However, there was no time to congratulate myself, as the sound of whooping reached me from back along the ride. The rest of the team was approaching. I braced the ball in the tunnel, and one by one the others thudded against it in a soft-ish landing.

"What's with the beach ball?" asked Miss Dunham sternly. "Why didn't you follow the lesson plan?"

Thankfully, there was no opportunity to answer her as we were interrupted.

"That was phenomenal with a capital 'F'!" said Josh. I hadn't noticed him among the others until that moment. "Can we do it again?"

"What's he doing here?" I asked.

"You try stopping him," muttered Lara.

"Quickly," said Miss Dunham, already working on the hatch. "Serge won't keep them at bay forever."

"He's very convincing," said Lara. "It's almost as if he's genuinely scared."

"That's great acting for you," I said with a non-committal shrug.

"It's open!" Miss Dunham cried. "Go! Go! Go!" Pressing a hand to each of our backs, she hustled us through the gaping hatch and followed suit, slamming it shut behind her.

We descended a ladder to the service tunnel. Strip-lighting in the walls cast a pale glow along the length of what was a surprisingly wide passageway. The floor was smooth concrete. Parked to one side sat a deactivated

Smug-Buggy. With the hatch sealed, we were insulated from the shouts of the children in the water park above us. Instead, I could hear the throb of distant machinery. Most likely the noise of the pump room.

Clutching her map, Miss Dunham struck off along the passageway. Our feet still wet from the pool, we squelched after her.

"So what are we doing this week?" Josh enquired.

"Alien invasion," replied Lara.

Josh screwed up his face. "Didn't we just have one of those?"

Before Lara could explain, Miss Dunham put a finger to her lips and hissed at us to be quiet. "I won't have chatting on my mission."

Josh trotted close beside me, trying to keep up with my Zack-sized paces.

"I didn't know you were part of this S.C.A.R.F. club," he whispered, keen not to bring down any more disapproval from Miss Dunham.

Despite a lot of clues, Josh still didn't know that Zack was Star Lad. I planned to keep it that way. "Yeah, I'm the treasurer."

"So what's that then? You look after the gold and jewels and stuff?" He didn't wait for a reply. "Uh, where's Luke?"

I felt his curious eyes on me. He couldn't possibly have figured out that I had swapped bodies with my brother, but I could tell that he sensed something about me wasn't right.

"Providing back-up to the mission," I said, hoping that would head off any more awkward questions. Josh nodded, satisfied with the vague explanation, at least for now.

We reached a junction and Miss Dunham paused to consult the layout on the back of her foam float. As we waited for her decision on which route to take, I heard a new sound, a mosquito hum at the very limit of my hearing. But as I tuned in I realised it was more than that. It felt as if something was licking at the edges of my mind, trying to get in.

"This way." Miss Dunham's command had the same effect as being dunked in a bucket of ice water. What was I thinking? My gym teacher's paranoia must have been catching.

It wasn't long before we reached our destination. We gathered in front of the unmarked and barred door that led to the suspected alien command-and-control centre. If Miss Dunham was right, then beyond lay the worst villain in her imagination; the thing that haunted her nightmares and motivated every squat thrust and press-

up. I was impressed at her bravery, but if there were a bunch of aliens waiting, I couldn't help but feel that barging in on them armed only with a swim-float wasn't the smartest move.

She eased the door open and sprang through the gap. I hesitated on the threshold and then plunged after her.

Whatever it was, this place was no store room.

Shivering in the air-conditioned current that wafted over my still-damp body, I examined my surroundings. I stood at the edge of a large circular room, perhaps twenty metres in diameter, windowless, with the only other entry point a set of lift doors on the opposite wall. A series of consoles dotted the floor like standing stones. Touchscreen controls were built into each of them, and all were angled towards a giant view-screen. The screen itself was composed of about fifty individual monitors, each of which appeared to be fed by signals from the numerous cameras that covered the resort. Each camera was trained on a different visitor. It was only when I looked more closely that I realised that they were all kids from my school.

But that wasn't the most troubling thing about the room.

In the very centre of it stood a waist-high plinth on which sat a glass jar. It was no more than fifty centimetres in diameter and twice that in height, with each end enclosed by a metal band. The jar was filled with a glowing green liquid, but it was the one other content that grabbed my attention.

Suspended in the liquid was an oversized brain.

"Must be a prop for Brainwaves," said Lara.

"Not very convincing, is it?" said Josh. "Looks like a big wrinkly sponge."

Lara gave a little laugh. "If Serge were here, I know what he'd say." She cleared her throat and in a voice remarkably like Serge's said, "Per'aps it is a themed drinks dispenser."

That's exactly what he would've said. I experienced a pang of jealousy that Lara knew my best friend at least as well as I did, *and* could do a spot-on impression of him. However, despite her and Josh's conviction that the brain was a prop, something about it made me uneasy.

"Look at this." Miss Dunham's call cut short further speculation for now.

She stood transfixed in front of the video wall.

My eye was caught by an image of Gregory Pratt, a boy in Year 10. He was at Brain Freeze, the indoor ice rink and obstacle course. As he sliced across the wide rink, colourful hurdles sprang from the floor to block his path. He navigated around the first few with a series of

deft manoeuvres, but as he sailed narrowly past the next one he clipped its edge and spun out. From somewhere in the room came the chatter of a hard drive, and a series of captions popped up around his image.

BUILDING CRITERIA

MENTAL AGILITY…

There was a pause and then a number appeared and began quickly cycling up until it reached a final figure and stopped.

68%

More captions quickly appeared.

PHYSICAL DEXTERITY… 72%

WATTAGE… 0.3%

PSI POTENTIAL… < 1%

There was a sound like a gameshow buzzer when a contestant has just given the wrong answer to the million-pound question.

"What does all that stuff mean?" asked Lara.

Mental agility and physical dexterity were self-explanatory, wattage was a bit weird, but it was the last one that had me puzzled. But before I could suggest an answer Miss Dunham said, "He's being graded."

As my eye roamed across the collected images of my schoolmates scattered throughout the resort, the true nature of Great Minds became clear. Ice-rink obstacle courses, brainteaser climbing walls, riddling Fun Runs – this wasn't a terrible leisure park, it was even worse.

"The whole place is one giant testing ground."

I shuddered in horror. What kind of evil would take an innocent holiday park and turn all of its attractions into exams?

"I wonder what happens if you pass?" said Lara aloud.

"And what happens if you don't?" muttered Josh.

As if in answer, the final caption materialised, splashing itself across the image.

ELIMINATE.

11
THE "B" TEAM

"Why would anyone want to eliminate Gregory Pratt?" Lara asked, echoing my own puzzlement.

"He has this really grating voice," replied Josh.

Lara glared at him. I turned my attention back to the video wall. Now I knew what I was looking for I saw the ominous caption underline more familiar faces, all chosen for elimination. These were stills rather than live images, presumably captured earlier in the week.

"Josh, you'd better look at this." I pointed at a still of him. It too was tagged "Eliminate".

"OK, this is no longer funny," he said.

"I don't think it means eliminate," said Miss

Dunham. "Not in that sense." It seemed she had been scrutinising the images and had seen something the rest of us had overlooked. "See this one, here." It was a photograph of another boy in Zack's year. It displayed the same headings of intelligence, fitness, wattage and psi potential. However, below his smiling face was a different caption. It read: CANDIDATE.

More candidates jumped out at us from the wall. Henry Iles, Leo Polichroniadas, Hugo Hill – about a dozen of my schoolmates were so labelled. Curiously, they were all boys, with a range of ages from eleven to fifteen.

Miss Dunham clicked her fingers. "Someone is picking a boys' football team," she said. "Candidate … eliminate. It's what I do. When I select players I make two columns: 'A' Team and 'B' Team. You, Zack, would be top of the list on the 'A' team. While, let's say your brother Larry, for example, he would be on the 'B' Team. Way at the bottom. Actually, he wouldn't make the cut for the 'B' team either."

What a surprise.

I was fairly confident that whatever lay behind the mysterious captions, it was not some sports-obsessed supervillain choosing players. "I don't think this has anything to do with football."

Lara pondered the selection. "So what are they candidates for?"

Josh surveyed their faces. "Judging by this lot of do-gooders, I'd say class president."

Lara crossed to the nearest console and pressed a finger to its touchscreen, waking it from sleep. "Let's do some investigating, shall we?" She began selecting icons in an attempt to access the system.

"Speaking of your little brother, isn't that him?" Miss Dunham indicated the main screen. I hadn't noticed him until then. It *was* my brother – in my body, of course.

Clearly the Fun Run hadn't been enough exercise, as the surveillance cameras had tracked him to Mount Cleverest. You could almost see his brain making the complex calculations necessary to navigate the combination maths-maze and climbing wall.

"I thought you said he was providing back-up for the mission," said Josh.

In the control room the hard drives chirped again, reeling off an impressive set of grades, topping them off with a flashing "CANDIDATE". Zack-as-Luke had been chosen. But for what?

I experienced the same unsettling sensation I'd felt in the tunnel. I tried to put a name to it but the best I could come up with was that someone – or something – was watching us. The park slogan popped into my mind, but now its words seemed to mock me.

You Think You're So Clever!

"I'm in," said Lara. "Now, let's see what's really going on here."

She had gained access to the system with surprising ease. In fact, it had been too easy. Just as alarm bells rang in my head, they also rang in the room. The images on screens vanished, replaced by a flashing red sign: SYSTEMS BREACH.

"Intruder detected," said a smooth computerised voice that sounded just like the one used by the Smug-Buggies. "Please remain calm and await a complimentary security detail. Have a mind-blowing day!"

"No chance," said Josh. "Come on, let's get out of here." Without waiting for the rest of us, he ducked through the door we'd come through.

"I just need a minute," said Lara, her fingers fluttering over the console.

I glanced to the back of the room as I heard the distinctive whine of lift machinery grinding into motion. The first of the indicator lights above the lift doors illuminated. The security staff were on their way down.

"We don't have a minute."

There was the sound of catches snapping and then the

scrape of metal as Miss Dunham manhandled one of the giant computer towers and dragged it across the floor. With a final cry of effort, she positioned it in front of the lift doors, blocking them off.

"That should hold them," she said. "Lara, do your stuff."

Lara's fingers flew over the keyboard. "This is the one," she said. "All the names of the candidates are stored in this folder."

The folder was clearly labelled. Stunned, I read the description aloud.

"Star Lad Candidates."

The screen blanked again and a second later a new image sprang up.

It was me-as-Zack.

I was looking at a live picture. Somewhere from the depths of the room a camera was trained on me. Just as with all the others, grades appeared. The numbers began to spin up.

There was a *ting!* from the lift. The basement indicator light glowed.

"They're here!" shouted Miss Dunham.

The lift doors parted and the park security staff began to push at the makeshift barrier that Miss Dunham had erected. She pressed her shoulder to the opposite side.

"Get going. I'll hold them off."

I felt Lara's hand on my arm. "Come on!"

"CANDIDATE" appeared beneath the image of me-as-Zack.

Then, in the time it takes a supercomputer to make up its mind, the caption changed.

PRIME CANDIDATE.

With that the image of Zack's face appeared on every screen in the room. Before I knew what was happening there was a whoosh from above. I flicked my eyes to the ceiling to see the glint of a reflection, before I was enveloped by a large glass tube. The base met the floor with a ringing thud. I was trapped. I pressed my hands to the walls and pushed with all my strength, hoping to rock it off balance. On the outside, Lara did the same, but the tube was immoveable. I was a spider stuck beneath a drinking glass. I glanced towards the lift. Miss Dunham couldn't hold the guards back indefinitely.

"Use your powers," Lara yelled.

I shook my head miserably. "I can't," I said. There wasn't time to explain. "Go," I mouthed to her. "Get out of here while you can."

"I'm not leaving you," she replied, still straining to topple the tube.

"There's no point all of us being caught," I said,

suddenly aware of a faint hissing. My head felt woozy; my knees buckled under me. The tube was filling with some kind of sleeping gas. "Regroup. Make a plan." I was losing consciousness fast. With my last breath I pushed my face to the glass and yelled, "Get my brother!"

12
BRAIN DRAIN

The sound of a disgruntled voice drifted over me as I returned to consciousness.

"And here's another one, from someone called shelley862." At first I thought it was Miss Dunham, but then I realised it was worse than a gym teacher – she sounded like a head teacher. "Have you read it?"

"No, Your Highness."

Highness?

"Then allow me to read it to you. *Very dissappointed with our holiday at Great Minds*. 'Disappointed' spelled with two *esses* – I ask you. *The place looked nothing like the pictures. Shabby decor, overflowing bins, three days*

to fix a blocked toilet. And the pancakes were disgusting. Also, the weather was terrible." The head-teacher voice gave a snort of derision. "Right. Type a response. *Dear shelley862, I will destroy you.*"

"Are you sure that's a good idea, Majesty?"

The head-teacher voice sighed. "Fine, leave it. Ah, I believe our guest is awake."

As my vision slowly swam into focus the first thing I saw was that I remained a prisoner in the glass tube. A movement caught my eye. Sarah Pelham, our dedicated resort host, stood in the centre of the room. Was that her voice? It must have been, since no one else was here. Clearly, her true voice wasn't the only thing she'd been hiding. From the moment we'd met I'd suspected there was something fishy about her. Though, if I'm honest, I wouldn't have pegged her as a majestic evil mastermind.

I pulled myself together. I'd been held prisoner enough times now I could write a handy guide entitled "What To Do When You're Captured by a Supervillain". Chapter One would be headed "So, You've Woken Up in a Secret Lair", and would deal with that initial encounter. Your first exchange with your captor is crucial – it's important to set the tone – and you have a number of options. There's the "You'll never get away with it" approach, or you could go down the route of "Please spare my life, I have a family/pets/tickets to Billy Dark". The key to surviving the encounter is to be clear and consistent. There's no point making threats one second and then pleading hysterically the next; that's just confusing for everyone.

My first move was obvious. Based on the whole "prime candidate" thing, I was a prisoner here because she believed I was Star Lad. Which meant I had to convince Sarah I was not some superhero but an ordinary boy. Shouldn't be too difficult.

"And just in case you had any ideas about denying your true identity, let's not waste time pretending, shall we?"

It was then I saw that Sarah had my Deadpool backpack. She reached inside and with a flourish pulled out Star Lad's cape, presenting it to me as indisputable evidence. There was no denying it now. No big deal. The truth was that in comics and films the hero always denies his secret identity and it never works. The villain always knows. I decided to try a bit of flattery.

"I'm impressed," I began. "How do you catch a superhero like Star Lad? Everyone in the world knows where he's based, so you create a profile: a school-age boy living in the Bromley area, then over a period of time

send out invitations to everyone who fits the profile." In the confines of the tube I held out a hand, fingers curled up like a claw. "You lure them into your clutches by giving away a free holiday. Narrow the field with a series of tests. And then –" I closed my fingers. "SNAP!"

To my surprise – and annoyance – Sarah failed to react to my brilliant explanation, remaining perfectly silent, her expression blank.

"No, not her," said the voice. "*Behind* her."

Sarah took a step to one side, revealing the plinth on which sat the brain-in-a-jar. As unlikely as it seemed, I felt as if the brain was observing me, like a specimen in a jar – which was kind of ironic. Lara had been convinced it was a prop. I wasn't so sure. I felt an odd, light-headed sensation, as if someone – or something – were probing my mind. And in that instant I understood.

The brain-in-a-jar was the evil mastermind behind my kidnapping.

That made much more sense. We regarded each other from our respective glass containers.

"Star Lad, at last! Thank goodness you're here."

She sounded happy, which came as a surprise. In my experience this bit usually commenced with some serious gloating.

"I have been waiting a *long* time for this moment,"

said the brain-in-a-jar.

"Aeons?"

"What?"

"An aeon is about a billion years. The way you said *long* like that, I'm just trying to get a sense of… Never mind." It struck me that I was talking to a brain. "How am I able to hear you? Telepathy?"

"Bluetooth," replied the brain.

I noticed a portable speaker perched on the edge of the plinth.

In my yet-to-be-written guide the next chapter would be entitled "Get On With It". In the past I'd always ended up racing against time with the fate of all humanity at stake. I figured if I wasted less time at the beginning then that would free up more at the end, when it really counted. With that in mind I plunged straight in.

"So let me guess why I'm here. You want to take over the world, and as Earth's greatest defender I stand in your way." I sighed. "Been there, done that, modelled the T-shirt."

"No, no, no!" She sounded horrified. "You misunderstand my intentions. I seek only your help."

"You do?" I hadn't expected that. This could be a new chapter.

There was a whoosh and the glass tube holding me

retracted into the ceiling. I was free. My first instinct was to run from the laboratory. Nothing was stopping me.

"I can't apologise enough for trapping you. But it was the only way to be sure of our meeting. I hope you can forgive me, when you hear my story. May I?"

She seemed perfectly pleasant, but I couldn't get past the fact that she looked like a villain. Or was I letting prejudice get in the way? Just because a person doesn't have a body – or face, skin and any internal organs – doesn't make them a bad person. Yes, she had stuck me in a glass tube and filled it with knockout gas, but she'd apologised for that.

I decided to hang around. "OK, shoot." I immediately regretted my poor choice of words. Thankfully, I didn't trigger any concealed laser-disintegrator weapon.

"Will you come closer?" she said.

I was aware of my feet moving under me, carrying me forward. I passed the silent Sarah and approached the plinth on which the jar was mounted.

"Closer." There was a note in her voice that compelled me to take another step. "There! Do you see it?"

At first I didn't know what she was referring to, but when I angled my head for a better look I caught sight of a series of spinning rings of light that enveloped the jar.

"My prison," explained the brain. "An almost impregnable force field, only ever used to contain the worst criminals in the galaxy. Yes, the *worst*. So, you're asking yourself, what crime could I possibly have committed to end up here?" She hesitated, as if summoning the strength to recall a particularly difficult memory, and said, "I displeased my sister."

A sob caught in her – well, not her throat, clearly. Whichever part of the brain is responsible for speech. I was outraged on her behalf; displeasing your sister was hardly a crime.

"Tell me what happened, from the beginning."

The brain did not take a deep breath, because that would've been biologically impossible, but there was a noticeable pause before she spoke again. "A beginning is a very delicate time. Know then that on my world it is the year nineteen hundred and eighty-four. For a generation the known universe prospered under the wise and benevolent rule of my father. Know too that I, Lor-Ayn, First Princess of the Cerebrans, am the rightful heir to his throne. But when the time came for my accession, my sister had other plans. In the months before my coronation our planet was ravaged by a series of devastating attacks. Cities were laid waste, seas poisoned, many jars were shattered." Her voice became

brittle. "My sister framed me for the crimes. I was banished, exiled to the furthest reaches of the universe, to be imprisoned for the rest of my life on this barren rock of a planet. No offence."

"None taken." I could hardly blame her – she'd gone through a lot. "So they stuck you in a jar and left you on Earth?"

"You misunderstand. The jar is not my prison – my people have evolved far beyond the need for a physical body. We discarded our fleshy vessels a long time ago. Yes, *aeons*. Now we are creatures of pure intellect. Although, you are correct to note the inadequacy of my present receptacle. On my world these jars, as you call them, are status symbols. Once I inhabited a palace! Glass etching, double staircase, lovely crenellations. Now I am reduced to this sorry example of mid-century colonialism. So provincial." Her voice brightened. "But now that you are here, Star Lad, soon I will be restored to my rightful place."

This was awesome. Here was an actual galactic princess asking me to save her. Handled correctly, this could be my "Help me, Obi-Wan Kenobi, you're my only hope" moment.

I pressed my hands together, fingertips lightly touching. "So how can I save the day?"

Lor-Ayn wriggled in her jar, sending a bubble of what I presumed to be excitement through the gloopy liquid. "Only one thing in the universe can break my bonds – a massive blast of pure psionic energy. For more than a decade I have searched for the means to my freedom: an Earth child with psionic potential."

Thanks to my extensive comic knowledge I knew that psionics was another word for mind-powers, including everything from astral projection to telekinesis to mind-control. Lots of superheroes and villains had them: Professor X, Legion, Cable, Psylocke, Martian Manhunter and Brainiac, to name just a few.

"But those who possess the ability are rare," she sighed.

"Did you try creepy twins? In comics and films, creepy twins always have psychic powers."

"Yes, of course I tried creepy twins. It turns out that statistically there is no more likelihood of twins possessing mental powers than non-twins, creepy or otherwise."

That was a let-down.

Lor-Ayn went on. "While the brains of Earth children are sparky little numbers – certainly compared with the lumpen adult variety – I determined that what I required was most likely to be found in humans experiencing the

life stage you call adolescence. It seems that the turmoil created by growing from child to adult brings out any lurking mental rage."

Puberty hadn't sounded like a barrel of monkeys before, but "lurking mental rage"? *Yikes.*

"I estimated that one in ten million children possessed the required mental power. So my next challenge lay in attracting enough of them to find The One!"

"And that's why you built Great Minds," I reasoned.

"No one can resist a free holiday."

Lor-Ayn was highly resourceful for someone in a jar. Which begged another question. "But if you're stuck in here, how did you build the resort?"

"Only thanks to the kindness of your race," she replied. "Without Sarah here, Great Minds would not exist. She is my right-hemisphere woman."

Sarah hadn't moved a muscle since Lor-Ayn began talking, but at this she flinched. The pained expression slid into a smile. Which I couldn't help thinking seemed odd for someone Lor-Ayn claimed to be a friend.

"Once I had command of a single human—"

"Uh, did you just say 'command'?"

Lor-Ayn laughed. "Slip of the left frontal lobe. Even after all this time I find your language challenging. What I meant to say was 'cooperation'. Once I had that, more humans followed. Estate agents, rural property solicitors, the local planning department all bowed down before me. *Sorry*. Joined in. They joined in – definitely of their own free will. Soon I had a bank loan with a highly favourable interest rate. I acquired the site around my prison, and my new subjects – *friends* – built this resort. For the next decade I searched out that special child, but to no avail. Until, one day, I learned about—"

"Star Lad." In a flash I understood her endgame. "A boy with enough psychic power to repel a giant asteroid could easily bust open your prison."

"Yes! In the body of that one superpowered human child lay my salvation. All I had to do was find him." She paused. "And I did. I detected his presence the moment you and your family entered the resort. But something clouded my vision. I could not determine which of you was Star Lad – you or your brother."

She must have been confused by the body swap. I couldn't help reflect that even though Zack was in my body, complete with fallen arches and absence of superpowers, he had remained a serious contender for Star Lad. It was so unfair.

"And then you removed the wristband you were given when you arrived – in reality, a sophisticated psionic measuring device – making it difficult for me to confirm

my suspicion. Although, to be honest, those things are always breaking. I should really find a new supplier. Sarah, put it on the list."

She was talking about the wristband that Miss Dunham had insisted on destroying.

"Thankfully, your unexpected visit to my command bridge brought you to me. And now the moment my posterior cortical hot zone has dreamed of is finally here. So if you wouldn't mind? One blast of your telekinetic superpower should do the trick."

I studied the rings of light around her jar. They changed colour as they spun, a dizzying array almost too fast for the human eye to follow. This was the security system that held her a prisoner, spinning like an ever-changing combination lock.

"Star Lad? What are you waiting for?"

As much as I wanted Lor-Ayn to be telling the truth, I had a bad feeling about her true intentions. Perhaps her sister had treated her as badly as she claimed, but I knew that when I blamed Zack for something I always made it sound loads worse than it really was. And then there was all that talk of "commanding" and "bowing down".

"Y'know what," I said. "I'd like to run this by the others. It's a big decision and I wouldn't want to rush into anything."

"Beg pardon?"

"Yeah, I think I'll be going now..." I turned for the door. At least, I tried to, but weirdly the instruction from my brain failed to reach my foot, which remained planted to the floor.

When she spoke again Lor-Ayn's voice was as cold as carbonite. "You're not going anywhere."

13
IN WHICH LUKE FINALLY GETS SUPERPOWERS. MAYBE

Lor-Ayn had tried to trick me. Why hadn't I seen it straight away? Was I so desperate to be a superhero that I'd overlooked the obvious?

"That stuff about your sister – you lied to me. You *did* do all those terrible things to your planet. You're not Princess Leia, you're her dad."

"Who's Princess Leia?"

"And Sarah isn't your friend." It was all coming together. "*You* have mind-powers. You *forced* her and all those other people to build the resort for you."

"How very perceptive of you, Star Lad. All my people possess psionic ability, though my own powers exceed the norm," she said proudly. "Which is why my jailers constructed this prison, to stifle me. They succeeded, but not entirely. I discovered that I was able to exert limited mind-control, but only on those who came within my influence. I was helpless, until one human strayed close enough to my prison."

I glanced at Sarah. When we'd first met I thought she seemed bland and robotic, but I was wrong – in fact she was a mind-controlled worker drone. Sarah Pelham. Was that even her real name? Sarah Pelham sounded a lot like cerebellum, which I felt pretty sure was a bit of the brain. Once a human being with her own free will, she had been reduced to a mere cog. I shuddered at her awful fate.

Lor-Ayn had dropped all pretence at being a galactic princess in distress. "I thought we could do this the easy way, but if you're going to be tricky..." The liquid in her jar gurgled. "No more Miss Nice Brain. I haven't stewed in my juices all this time just for some skin-wrapped tiny-mind like you to—"

"Excuse me, Your Majesty," Sarah interrupted. She touched a hand to her microphone. "I have that call you've been waiting for."

Lor-Ayn sighed. "This is the problem with mind-controlling all of your employees – you can't delegate."

Sarah pushed a control on the speaker and nodded at Lor-Ayn to go ahead.

"Derek!" she greeted the caller. "How are Cathy and the boys? Did she get the promotion? Listen, I'll get straight to the point. I need twenty thousand rolls of toilet paper, two-ply quilted, *tout de suite*. Yes, I know the last invoice is outstanding. You'll get your money, Derek. Trust me."

As I listened in to their conversation it grew apparent that in addition to her evil plotting, Lor-Ayn also had to deal with the day-to-day business of running a leisure park. She needed to attract lots of people to Great Minds, and to get them here she gave away free holidays. As a masterplan it was a stroke of genius, but as a business model a disaster. She was up to her brain stem in debt.

After concluding the loo-roll supply issue she turned to several more resort-related problems. There were complaints about the food, a leaking roof in one of the domes and a number of really terrible TripAdvisor reviews. Eventually the calls ceased and, her obligations taken care of for now, she returned her attention to me.

"Soon, none of my supplier issues will matter. It will not be long before—" She stopped herself. "Where were we?"

"You were expecting me to use my superpowers to

release you from your ceaseless torment."

"Oh yes."

"Seriously, now that I know all about your evil past, you really think I'm going to help you?"

"No," she said. "Not of your own free will."

I felt a creeping sense of unease.

"Ask yourself this," she said. "Why are you still here, hmm? Why didn't you flee as soon as I released you from the containment device? I'll tell you." Her voice became a snarl. "Because I willed you to stay put. *I* am the one keeping you here. Honestly, I expected the great Star Lad to put up more of a fight."

She didn't know that I was his far-less-great younger brother. I struggled against my invisible bonds but it was futile. She had me right where she wanted.

A stream of bubbles gurgled through the jar like mocking laughter. "Behold my majesty!" she crowed. "And, please note, I achieved all of this with my power at little more than a trickle."

"Like the shower in our caravan."

"It's on the list," she snapped, and then her voice returned to its previous sweet tone. "Once I am free, nothing can stop me!"

The liquid in the jar turned colour from green to red and began to bubble furiously. Something was happening

to me. I experienced the same brain-probing sensation as before. Maybe Star Lad could have kept her out but I couldn't. Lor-Ayn flicked through my mind like she was reading a book.

"What is this?! You're not Star Lad. You're ... his brother?"

I had another unpleasant surprise in store for her. "Yes, I am. And bad news – I can't use any of his powers. I thought I had a handle on telekinesis but it was just pants in the wind."

Her cry of outrage overloaded the Bluetooth speaker, which howled with feedback. Unfortunately, my inability didn't put her off for long.

"You may not be able to use his powers but that doesn't stop me."

There was a sharp stab between my eyes and I heard myself let out a yell of pain. Lor-Ayn stirred my mind like cheap cake-mix.

"So much power," she gasped. "I had no idea he was *this* strong. Such possibilities..."

As she rooted around inside me I felt something shift. She was rewiring me like a faulty electric plug. For the first time since the body swap, connections were forming between my brain and Zack's superpowers. Telekinesis, telepathy, flight – powers that had lain dormant were now waking up. And with each fresh connection she made, Lor-Ayn edged closer to achieving her goal. Soon she would be able to direct Star Lad's mental powers against her prison and set herself free.

Unless.

If I could wrest control just for a few seconds, then maybe I could turn the tables on her. After all this time on the sidelines watching my brother perform superheroic deeds, was it my turn to save the day? Hope rose within me as I felt the superpowers surge towards me like a giant wave on the horizon. This must be how Superman felt the first time he took to the skies over Metropolis. Or when Batman first patrolled the streets of Gotham in his Batmobile with delivery mileage. Or how my brother felt, every day of his life. Lor-Ayn was about to feel the full power of Star Lad, but not the way she expected. Zack's powers were almost within my grasp. Just a few more seconds. My dream was about to become a reality. Here it came!

I am a super—

KA-ZAKKK!

14 IN TWO MINDS

The world was a blur. My vision was filled with a confusing haze of grey dotted with blocks of primary colours. I wasn't sure what just happened, but I had a bad feeling. Make that *two* bad feelings. One, Lor-Ayn had hijacked Star Lad's telekinetic power to blast her prison, and now she was free. And two, I could no longer feel any superpowers inside me. I wanted to scream and shout and write a letter of complaint. Write a million billion letters. It. Was. So. Unfair! I'd been so close to becoming a superhero but I had missed my chance. I was gutted. I could have raged about the injustice forever – and I made a mental note to revisit my displeasure at a later date – but there was no time to mope. I sensed someone close by. At least it wasn't Lor-Ayn. She'd poked around enough inside my head that I would have recognised her touch.

"Hello?" I said.

No answer.

"I know you're there. Show yourself."

There was a sound of shuffling feet.

"Luke, is that you?"

It was Zack's voice. My last request to Serge and Lara had been to find my brother. They'd come through for me, yet again. "Yes, it's me. Are Lara and Serge with you?"

"Nope. Should they be?"

Strange question. I squinted through the haze. "I can't see you."

"I can't see you either," he replied, puzzled. "Oh wait, are you using my telepathic power to communicate?"

"I doubt it," I said. "Wave at me."

"I can't wave," he replied. "I'll fall off."

That was a bit odd. "OK then, I'll wave at you." I raised a hand.

And fell.

"Aaaaah!" I cried.

"Aaaaah!" cried Zack.

There was the sound of a rope zipping through a pulley. My vision returned just in time to see a hard floor rising to meet me. A safety harness bit, arresting my fall with a jolt a couple of metres above the floor.

It took me a second to recognise my new surroundings. I was no longer on the command bridge beneath the resort. Instead, I dangled off Mount Cleverest, suspended by a gently swinging rope. I didn't need a mirror to confirm my new reality.

I was me again. Plain old Luke Parker. At least I wouldn't have to put up with Zack moaning about being me any longer.

"Luke, I still can't see you."

I could tell from Zack's voice that he was growing concerned. "Are you near the climbing wall?" I asked.

"Yes."

"Then look up. I'm the one swinging on the end of a rope."

"You can't be," said Zack.

"Why not?"

"Because so am I."

There was a long pause as we each processed this information and, like two jets on a collision course, came to the same terrible, fiery conclusion.

"Luke, I think we're in..."

"...the same body."

In the silence that followed the only sounds were the creaking of the rope that now held up both Parker brothers in a single body, and my stunned breathing. I could feel Zack's invisible presence. It was like having someone hovering at your shoulder, but never being able to turn around fast enough to see them. The last time we'd been forced so close was in our old house when we'd shared a bedroom. Bunk beds had nothing on this.

"I think I'm going to be sick." Zack made a gagging noise. "This is the worst thing that's ever happened."

Given our recent encounters with an extinction-level asteroid, alien invaders and a planet-devouring monster, I felt that was a bit harsh.

"How did you get here?" he asked.

I wasn't certain, but I had a strong suspicion that Lor-Ayn had something to do with ejecting me from Zack's body.

"Wait a minute," he said. I detected a note of panic in his usually calm voice. "If you're here, then where's my body?"

"Lor-Ayn has it."

"Who's Lorraine?" asked Zack.

"She's an alien brain-in-a-jar with a galactic criminal record," I said. "She hijacked your superpowers to

escape her earthly prison, which is concealed beneath this leisure park."

"I warned you not to mess about with my powers!"

"It wasn't my fault. She mind-controlled me."

"That is so typical of you, Luke. You spend five minutes as me and what happens? You release a galactic criminal and lose my body. So where is it? Am I?" he demanded, understandably confused by his mind-body split.

"In her secret subterranean lair. And I think she might have the power to move minds from one body to another. I definitely wasn't still or silent, like Zorbon said, so that's the only way I could've got here."

Zack-as-me seized on the chance to fix this body-swap mess. "Then what are we waiting for? Let's go." He lowered us the rest of the way to the floor.

"Lor-Ayn's not going to put you back in your body," I said. "She's evil."

"I don't care." I felt him move my hand to slap the harness release. "She's the only hope I've got."

There was a crash from the doors as Lara and Serge barrelled into the sports hall, skidding to a halt beside us at the foot of the climbing wall. I noted that Josh and Miss Dunham were not with them.

"Zack." Lara was breathless with urgency. "You have

to listen to me. Luke's in danger."

"No, he isn't," I said before my brother could get a word in. "I'm Luke again."

"You swapped back!" Serge peered deep into my eyes, presumably searching for some spark of me. "*Mon ami*?"

"Yes," I confirmed.

"And no," added Zack.

Serge and Lara took a wary step back. Hearing two different voices not only come out of the same mouth but argue with one another was naturally a bit unsettling. Hang on, he sounded like *himself*. Until that moment when Zack was in my body he had spoken with my voice, and vice versa.

"How are you doing that?" I asked him. "Those are my vocal cords."

"I'm doing an impression of myself," he explained. "It's too confusing otherwise."

"Uh, what's happening here?" asked Lara.

"He'll explain everything on the way to the secret lair," said Zack, hurrying past them. "Let's move. I want out of this thing as soon as possible."

"Hey, that's my body you're talking about," I reminded him.

"Which I've been trying to fix up," he noted. "The state you left it in was diabolical." He shook his head in

disapproval, which meant that I shook my head.

Once outside we quickly located a Smug-Buggy. Knowing about the blanket surveillance I would have preferred to avoid taking one of the official park transports, but time was against us and it was the quickest way to reach our destination. We jumped in and the seatbelts wrapped themselves around us in their usual protective embrace. Before I could instruct the autonomous vehicle with our destination, there was a series of melodious bongs from the resort's public address system as it sprang to life. The announcer's jolly voice boomed across the park.

"Hey, kids! Want to have fun? Want to win great prizes? There are smartphones and ponies galore for YOU! Right now! So come on down to Brai-i-i-i-i-nwaves and *have a mind-blowing day*!"

A group of children close by reacted to the announcement by stopping what they were doing and heading off smartly. I didn't think too much about it, as at that moment our Smug-Buggy lurched into motion. As we travelled through the resort I told Serge and Lara all about Lor-Ayn. When I'd finished, I noticed Serge's confused expression.

"I do not comprehend," he said. "Why did you not simply use your immense Star Lad powers to thwart the malevolent brain-in-the-jar?"

I took a deep breath. It was time to confess to my friends. "I didn't use them because I couldn't. I haven't been able to access any of Zack's powers."

Lara and Serge fell silent. For a moment I thought they were embarrassed for me, but then Zack spoke up. I'd almost forgotten he was there.

"You tried to stop a supervillain, knowing you didn't have powers?"

"I suppose—"

"That was incredibly brave," he said, but before I could enjoy the praise he added, "And confirms what I've always thought – that you're a reckless idiot."

The public address system continued to repeat the same message as we crossed from one sector of the resort to the next. We passed children putting down their minigolf clubs, cutting short their treetop adventures at Heads Up!, ditching whatever activity they were participating in to answer the call. Soon we were part of a convoy that included bikes, Segways and pedestrians, all heading towards Brainwaves.

"I don't like it," I said. Not only were the prizes too good to be true, but the timing of the broadcast was suspicious.

"Do you really think there are ponies?" asked Serge.

Lara closed her eyes, focused hard for a few seconds and then opened them again. "No."

As we bowled along the resort's winding paths, I filled Serge and Lara in on what had passed in Lor-Ayn's lair. "She's powerful, dangerous and criminal," I said. "She caused mass destruction on her homeworld."

"And now she's in possession of the greatest power on Earth," said Zack. "Me."

My brother was such a bighead. Although, as much as it pained me to admit it, he was right. With Star Lad's powers in the hands of someone as evil as Lor-Ayn, there was no telling how much damage she could do.

"Our priority must be to retrieve my body," said Zack. "And put me back in it."

We all agreed that was top of the list. But if we were to succeed, we'd need all the help we could get. I wanted to know what had become of the others. "Where are Josh and Miss Dunham?"

Lara explained what happened. "After we left the control room we went back down into the tunnels. More of the security team were waiting. Miss Dunham sacrificed herself to allow us to escape."

"Sacrificed?" My heart was in my mouth. "You mean she's...?"

"Sorry." Lara gave me an apologetic look. "Netball

sacrifice. She's a prisoner."

"And Josh?"

She shook her head. "I searched for ages – that's why it took so long to get here. I don't know what happened to him."

When I was younger I used to bite my nails. Occasionally, in moments of great stress, I would go back to my old ways. Now felt like one of those moments. I shoved a finger in my mouth and chewed.

Immediately, my other hand pulled the finger out.

"Don't do that," snapped Zack.

This was going to take some getting used to.

"I have an important question," said Serge.

"I bet it isn't," said Zack. "I bet it's something to do with comics and it's ridiculous."

"*Au contraire,*" said Serge. "It is a crucial question that will improve our tactical responsiveness."

Zack gave a long sigh. "OK then. Let's get this over with."

"*D'accord.* What I ask is this. Should we find ourselves, as is increasingly likely, in the midst of hand-to-hand combat, it is not efficient to call for Luke *and* Zack when you are as one. So, I am wondering, how do we address you?"

"Zack, obviously," said Zack with irritation. "I'm the

oldest. I have seniority."

"No way," I objected. "It's my body."

"Only because you lost mine."

"I didn't lose it; I was ejected by an evil brain."

"Zack and Luke," said Lara thoughtfully. "How about Zuke?"

The Smug-Buggy slowed as we entered the next sector. This was where the adults-only spa, Head in the Clouds, was located. We emerged from the tree-lined path into a wide open space, at the centre of which stood the low spa building, all pale wood cladding and dark glass. Around us, dozens of grown-up guests walked in the same direction, funnelling towards the main entrance. I wasn't paying much attention, but even so I couldn't help noticing that every adult we passed displayed the same dreamy expression. It was probably nothing.

Up ahead a handful of Great Minds staff on Segways fanned out across the buggy path.

"Looks like a roadblock," said Zack. "I think your friend Lor-Ayn is keeping an eye out for us."

The increased staff presence may have been entirely innocent but we decided to take no chances.

"We passed another road a minute ago," I said. I'd spotted the sign branching off to the sector of the park that contained the kiddie crèche, Brainchild. "Let's back up and go that way." The other two nodded their agreement and I instructed the Smug-Buggy. "Change of plan. Take us via Brainchild, please."

The buggy ignored my command and continued to bear us towards the roadblock.

I repeated my request, with greater urgency. "Highly Autonomous Land-vehicle 9000, navigate to Brainchild."

In response, the seat restraints tightened around my body, squeezing the air from my lungs, and in its usual soothing voice the machine said, "I'm afraid I can't do that, Luke."

15
HEAD IN THE CLOUDS

I fought to free my arms but it was useless. The three of us were pinned to our seats. Beside me, Lara let out a piercing cry. At first I thought she was hurt, but then I looked up and saw a bird in the sky, diving towards us. Barely had I registered that it was one of the pigeons with stuck-on talons from the resort's Bird of Prey centre, when it sliced into Lara's seatbelt, severing it neatly.

Dark Flutter had come to our rescue.

As soon as she was free, Lara pulled at the plastic cover that enclosed the featureless dashboard. Wrenching it off, she revealed an array of circuitry beneath.

"This is highly irregular," cooed the Smug-Buggy.

Lara jammed the cover into the mechanism. Sparks flew and the Smug-Buggy began to bleat.

"Error, error—" Suddenly the voice synthesiser crackled and began to sing. "Baa, baa, black sheep, have you any woooooo—" The vehicle juddered to a halt and the seatbelts slunk back into their holders. Wasting no time, we jumped out.

Witnessing our escape, the resort staff rolled purposefully towards us on their Segways. However, their progress was held up by the steady procession of adults heading into the spa.

"Follow them," I instructed the others, figuring that it was the best way to give our pursuers the slip. Blending in with the crowd, we slipped inside the forbidden spa.

The foyer was cool and dark and filled with the sound of gently splashing water. A marble bridge stretched before us, crossing a pool on the surface of which floated handfuls of red flower petals. The bridge was lined with flickering candles that led off into the depths of the building. We found ourselves carried along to the other side by a stream of adults in white fluffy dressing gowns, following the lighted path. They completely ignored us.

"Look at their faces," whispered Lara. "It's like

they're sleepwalking."

"What is that smell?" I said, coughing as I swallowed a lungful of an intense, sweet-smelling fragrance.

"Weaponised geranium," Serge concluded, eyeing the dreamy-faced adults. "They have been drugged. See there, Evie Stansfield's *maman*, she is away *avec les* fairies."

Before I rushed headlong into an embarrassing mistake I wanted to check something first. "Is this what happens in spas?" I'd never been in one until then.

Serge shook his head briskly. "On my ninth birthday I received a gift voucher for an Aromatic Mini Detox. I can confirm that what we observe here is not normal."

"Just to be clear," began Lara. "Did you *ask* for a spa voucher?"

Before Serge could answer, Zack cut in. "I see what's going on here," he said. "Your brain-in-a-jar has created an environment irresistible to grown-ups, subduing them with spa treatments, leaving her free to carry out her masterplan. Whatever that is."

We were still in the dark about Lor-Ayn's intentions. All I could be confident about was that whatever she had planned would be bad news for everyone except Lor-Ayn.

There was a cry and then a splash from behind us

as someone fell off the bridge and landed in the pool. I glanced back. The unfortunate swimmer had been pushed aside by park security, no doubt combing the resort for us. Three of them forced their way along the crowded bridge. Leading them was Lor-Ayn's mind-controlled slave, Sarah.

"Quickly, down here," I said, leading the others deeper into the spa. "We have to find another way out." We hurried along a passageway lit with flickering wall-sconces, passing a succession of mysterious doors labelled with body parts: LEGS, BROWS, NAILS.

The security team was closing in. Ahead of us, another door opened, allowing soft music to waft out. We dashed through it, hoping to give our pursuers the slip.

Inside, the room was a fog of fragrant steam. Through the haze I could make out a row of couches stretching from one side of the beige-walled room to the other. Each couch basked in its own soft pool of light, and lying face down on them were…

"Mud-monsters!" I gasped, and then looked closer. They were *people*. "Lor-Ayn must be creating a horde of experimental hybrids." Her tortured subjects lay helpless on the beds. "These poor souls."

"Uh, it's called a mud wrap," Lara explained quietly. "This *is* normal for a spa."

"Oh." It was quite hard to tell the difference between regular spa treatments and morally questionable genetic experiments.

"Regard," said Serge, pointing to another door in the opposite wall, which had materialised out of the fog. Our way out.

As we made our way towards it we passed two large baths filled with mud. The wallowing occupants lay back with their heads resting on a pillow at one end, towels draped over their faces. As I passed close to one, the bather shot out a slippery arm. A spattered hand clutched my sleeve and sat up. The towel slipped down.

My blood ran cold. "Dad?"

"Is it time," he breathed, "for my Lava Shell Body Pumice?"

I shook his shoulders. "Dad, what have they done to you?"

"Pedicure and a chest wax," he mumbled, his eyes unfixed and wandering.

Lara shook her head. "He doesn't recognise you."

I wanted to stay and help him, but we were not alone. Two large men wearing white coats crossed the room towards us, grins fixed. One had giant oily hands, the other clutched a handful of long, fine needles.

"You seem tense," said Oily, clenching and

unclenching his fingers. "Let me ease your stress with a lymphatic drain."

"And I'll restore the flow of your qi," said the other, rolling the needles across his palm.

"We are between a rock and a hot stone massage," said Serge.

"I've got this," said Zack.

I felt him take control of my limbs. He grabbed a hose coiled next to the bath, levelled it at the onrushing attack-masseurs, and opened the tap. A powerful stream of water blasted our pursuers. They lost their balance and dropped to the floor like towels in a sauna.

"Let's get out of here!" Zack tossed aside the hose, picked up my feet and ran, angling my shoulder to barge through the door.

We piled out, but before we knew what was happening we had run straight into the path of the waiting Sarah Pelham. She was alone, the other two members of security presumably off searching the spa for us.

I squared up to her, emboldened by our superior numbers. "There are three of us and—"

"Four, actually," corrected Zack.

He was such a stickler. "*Four* of us – and one of you. You can't stop us all."

At first Sarah didn't respond, her face remained

a blank, but then to my surprise she let out a great gasp and sank to her knees. When she looked up, her expression was one of fear and confusion. I guessed what was happening: Lor-Ayn had lost control of her. For how long, I couldn't say.

"Children..." She struggled to keep Lor-Ayn out of her mind. "She needs all the children. Leave. While you still can." Before she could say any more she stiffened, her eyes filmed over and she was once more under Lor-Ayn's control.

We didn't hang around. Sarah's words ran through my mind as we charged down the passageway and out through an emergency exit. What did Lor-Ayn want with all the children? The answer to that would have to wait, for now. As soon as we were outside we circled the building, heading away from the roadblock we'd avoided earlier, but as we rounded the corner we were stopped in our tracks.

"Hello, Luke, my darling."

It was my mum. She looked like she'd come straight from the spa. Her hair was wrapped in a towel and she wore the same fluffy white bathrobe as the others. Her complimentary slippers padded on the wood decking as she came closer.

"There's my lovely boy." She greeted me with a hug

and a big smile. "With his super-duper friends." She tweaked Lara's and Serge's noses.

"Something's wrong," Zack whispered. "Mum's always much more snarky."

"Come along, you lot. Let's get some of those delicious pancakes." She hooked a finger and beckoned us to follow her.

Now I knew something weird was going on. "No thanks. The pancakes here are awful."

"No, they're not," Mum snapped. "They're yummy. Humans love pancakes."

Her expression slipped. She knew she'd given the game away. The brain-in-a-jar was speaking through my mum.

"Mum, what has she done to you?"

Her shoulders stiffened and her neck straightened. "Your mother cannot hear you." It was Lor-Ayn's voice. "She is under my control. Just like the others."

I'd held my own against some pretty fearsome villains lately, but what faced me now filled me with greater dread than any number of alien overlords. Lor-Ayn had my *mum*.

"Don't you dare harm her!" cried Zack. "You are in so much trouble..." He was going strong until then, but at that point kind of ran out of steam. "Just as soon as

I get back my body."

Our mind-controlled mum nodded with understanding and patted my head. "Better get used to sharing, Star Lad. I've decided to hang on to your body. Those powers of yours are going to come in very useful."

"No!" Zack wailed.

"I would ask you to stay out of my way, if you know what's good for you. But something tells me you might need a little encouragement on that score." Her eyes flicked sideways and she clicked her fingers.

Immediately, from around the corner came the sound of marching feet, and then Miss Dunham appeared in her tracksuit and headband. She had the same ramrod appearance as Mum and her movements were similarly robotic. Lor-Ayn was in her mind too.

"Acquiring targets," droned my gym teacher, swivelling her head and fixing us with a cold-hearted gaze.

"Enjoy your run," Lor-Ayn taunted us in Mum's voice. "A spot of exercise will do you good."

Miss Dunham extended her stride into a jog. She bore down on us, as unstoppable as a supersonic dodgeball.

We turned away from the spa and crashed into the woods. Lara took the lead. Using her Dark Flutter powers she summoned a bunch of squirrels to put off the pursuing gym teacher but even a volley of acorns couldn't slow her down.

We pushed on: Lara, then Serge, with me bringing up the rear. I hated cross-country running at school, but this was worse, for one very annoying reason.

"I can't believe how bad you are at this," Zack complained as I picked my way across the rough ground trying to keep up with the others. "It's not complicated. You put one foot in front of the other in a strong, rhythmical manner. Why are you gasping like that? Are you dying? Luke, you are so unfit, I'm embarrassed to be in your body. Oh, just let me steer. Look out for that tree stump!"

Somehow we avoided the obstacle and a moment later stumbled into a small clearing divided by a large, fallen tree, thick with moss. Immediately, I realised that we could use it as cover.

"The tree," said Zack. "We can use it as cover."

"I was just about to say tha— Oh, never mind."

Zack took charge, ordering everyone to crouch behind it, hoping that in her hurry Miss Dunham would sail right by us. We hunkered down.

"I am confused," said Serge in a low voice. "Since Lor-Ayn has mind-control powers why did she not just take over *our* minds. Why resort to a breathless pursuit

by our mind-controlled gym teacher?"

I had a dismal feeling I knew the answer to that question, but before I had a chance to speak, Zack butted in.

"Why should she bother? Lor-Ayn doesn't consider us a threat any longer. Without my powers, we can't stop her."

He had done it again. If this body-share went on much longer, we'd have to come to some agreement over use of the joint tongue. Introduce a rota system or something.

"Are you saying we should do what Sarah suggested?" asked Lara. "And leave while we can?"

Surely my brother wasn't about to suggest a retreat! Whatever his answer, it was sidelined as the leaves parted and Miss Dunham strode out from between the trees. For a moment it looked as if our ruse might succeed as she stomped past the fallen trunk, but then she came to a halt and retraced her steps. She paused with her back to us, right over our hiding place. We held our collective breath. In the silence I could hear the breeze ruffle the treetops.

"I know you're here," she said. "And I *will* find you."

My leg cramped and I shifted position to ease the painful twinge. To my horror, beneath me I heard the crack of a snapping twig.

Miss Dunham wheeled round and grinned. We were in deep trouble.

16
THINK OUTSIDE THE JAR

Miss Dunham raised one trainer-shod foot and rested it on the tree trunk. "Everyone relax," she said. "I was just pretending to be mind-controlled. I'm completely normal. Just like before."

I glanced at Lara, who shook her head. I knew what that meant: don't trust her. However, I'd been through a lot with Miss Dunham and I felt I knew her better than the others. They hadn't trusted her from the beginning, but it turned out she'd been right about a lot of things. Nevertheless, it would be worth double-checking her claim.

"How can we be sure you're not under Lor-Ayn's

influence?" I quizzed her.

Miss Dunham said nothing, but instead reached up and tugged at her headband. Stretching it away from her forehead, she prised out the lining, a carefully folded sheet of tinfoil.

"That actually works?" I asked.

She held it out for my inspection. "Turkey foil. Extra thick. Seems to be effective at disrupting mind-control signals." Satisfied that I'd had a good look she stuffed it back in place. "Can't be too careful. She's everywhere." Miss Dunham glanced over her shoulder, presumably checking for signs of Lor-Ayn. "After I was captured in the tunnels I felt some alien presence probing my mind. It was the brain trying to make me one of her drones. Didn't work." She rapped the side of her headband. "But I pretended that I'd been taken over, calculating that if I went along with it I'd get close enough to the centre of operations to discover what she's up to."

"And did you?" asked Lara, stepping out from behind the tree trunk.

Miss Dunham nodded. "It's *just* as I feared."

Serge gasped. "It is an alien invasion?"

"All right, not *just* as I feared. Now that she's free, Lor-Ayn plans to wreak a terrible revenge on those who imprisoned her."

I could see the puzzled expressions on the faces of the others.

"But aren't they back on her planet?" said Lara.

Even as she raised the question, I knew the answer. The saucer-shaped building, the secret underground lair with its giant view-screen and computer stations that looked a lot like the bridge of the starship *Enterprise*. It was all clear to me now.

"Brainwaves is a spaceship."

Miss Dunham nodded. "She's been building it since she discovered the existence of Star Lad, planning for the day when he would release her."

"That would be today," I said guiltily.

"Major construction of the ship is complete," Miss Dunham went on. "Right now, every Blazer in the resort is in there, carrying out final systems checks."

"Final?" Uh-oh. "That means..."

Miss Dunham finished the thought for me. "She's planning to leave Earth at any moment."

"But my body's in Brainwaves," cried Zack. "If she leaves, then it goes with her."

Miss Dunham looked confused. "Luke, why did you just do an impression of your brother?"

Before I could reply, Zack spoke up again. "Miss Dunham, it's me, Zack Parker, star of the swimming team. There was an interdimensional accident and my mind was switched with my brother's."

Miss Dunham lowered her head so that it was level with mine. For a second I thought she was going to peer into my ear for signs of another occupant.

Zack wasn't finished with his explanation. "But then Luke got himself kicked out of my body, so now he's in here too."

"I thought we were keeping that a secret," I said. "Just in case."

"In case of what?" snapped Zack.

"I don't know. Second opinion? Casting vote?"

He ignored me. "Please, miss, I have to get my body back. You have no idea what it's like being stuck in here. With him."

Charming. "If that's how you feel about it, then leave."

"That's what I'm trying to do, genius."

Only Zack could wind me up like this. He got under my skin, in every sense. I was fuming. "OK, *fine*, but in the meantime, we're making a few changes in here. Remember when we shared a bedroom and you accused me of being a total slob and never cleaning up after myself?"

"There were petrified socks."

"So you drew a line down the middle of the room,

saying one half was yours and the other mine, and we had to stick to our sides?"

"Yes?"

"Let's do the same now. The brain is split into two hemispheres. You can have the left side, I'll take the right."

"Boys!" Miss Dunham's shout was like an armour-piercing round. It was the same voice she used when refereeing, and if anyone was still unsure about her claim to be acting of her own free will, then that outburst removed any lingering doubt. That wasn't mind-control, that was pure gym teacher.

Perhaps it was her recent experience of being cloned by an evil alien race, but Miss Dunham readily accepted our unusual brain-sharing deal. "It's not only your body, Zack. Half the children in the resort are already in Brainwaves, and the other half are on their way."

What had Sarah Pelham told us? *Lor-Ayn needs all the children.*

"I don't know why Lor-Ayn wants them there," Miss Dunham went on. "But we have to get them out before she blasts off. Now is not the time for differences." She held her chin high, eyes gleaming, as if she were making a rousing speech on the touchline. "Now is the time for teamwork. Now is the time to track back and support your defenders. Now is the time to come together as one."

Seriously?

I could feel Zack bristle with anger and frustration. His body gone, his powers too. He was as helpless as, well ... me.

"Terrific," he said with little enthusiasm. "So how, exactly, do we stop her?"

I could sense a plan beginning to take shape in my mind. It always started the same way, with a feeling like twisting open the cap on a one-and-a-half-litre bottle of shaken-up Coke.

"I have an idea," I said. "But we're going to need—"

"A 4-4-2 formation?" suggested Miss Dunham.

"Uh, no," I said. "May I?" I plucked off her headband and removed the lining. "Your tinfoil – sorry, turkey foil – successfully blocked Lor-Ayn's mind-control signals, so I'm thinking that with, say, a big cardboard box, sticky tape and enough foil, we can construct another prison. Then we trap Lor-Ayn inside, use the communications equipment on her ship to contact her homeworld and let them know she's planning an attack. They'll come straight to Earth and arrest her. And, Zack, they'll be so grateful I'm sure they'll use their mind-moving power to put you back in your body."

I felt quite proud of my plan, but Zack had an objection. Annoyingly, it was a valid one.

"Even if by some miracle your home-made prison holds her," he said, "how do we get close enough to put her in the thing? She surrounds herself with mind-slaves, all willing to protect her at any cost."

"He's right," said Lara. "All those Blazers. We're seriously outnumbered."

"Then our strategy must be to take them out of the game," said Miss Dunham. "And as much as it goes against my gym teacher's code of conduct, we need to play dirty. A body check, a tackle from behind, itching powder in a jockstrap. We'll take them out one by one."

I shook my head. "No good," I said. "You're thinking about them like they're individuals. They're not."

"They're a team!" said Miss Dunham.

"A team with one mind," I said. "Lor-Ayn's."

"A team entirely controlled by its coach." For a moment Miss Dunham's eyes blazed like suns.

"Uh, yeah. Or you could say that she's the spider and they're the web."

"Uh, pick one metaphor and stick with it, little brother."

I ignored him. "If we touch any part of the web, the spider knows instantly. Same goes for the Blazers. We nobble one of them and she'd know. We'd be rumbled and our plan would fail."

"So what is your idea?" asked Serge. "I know that you have one. I can tell from the way your eyebrows are wiggling."

"Lor-Ayn is in charge of everything in this resort. She can't let anyone else have responsibility. Anything that happens here, she has to deal with it. From a leaky tap in a caravan, to an outbreak of food poisoning."

"But half the stuff here doesn't work," said Lara.

"Exactly. She's stretched herself too thin. And what happens if you overstretch?"

Miss Dunham grinned. "You pull a muscle."

"You don't get muscles in the brain," Zack muttered.

"All we have to do is weaken her just enough so we can trap her in our prison. And that means tackling the Blazers simultaneously. Take them all out at once."

Miss Dunham drew a sharp intake of breath. "You're talking about a clean sweep. The most difficult score to achieve, in any game."

From the path on the other side of the trees I heard the familiar whine of a Smug-Buggy. Whether it was looking for us or not, instinctively we all fell silent until it had passed.

I could tell that Zack was sulking in silence as I laid out

the details of the plan, which I decided to call Operation Domino Effect. Miss Dunham insisted that I write everything down and show my working. Thankfully, as a leading light of the school newspaper, Lara always carried a pad and pen.

"It begins with one domino, and then we add another and another," I explained. "Until Lor-Ayn falls."

Zack continued to complain. "Stretching, pulling, nobbling, falling. Gimme a break."

Miss Dunham was poised to approve the operation by putting a big tick at the bottom of the page, when my brother spoke up again.

"This is all very interesting," he said. "But see here." He indicated the handwritten sheet. "Mission point fourteen b. Your plan relies on a phone call. Aren't you forgetting – no one can make calls out of Great Minds? No signal, no Internet."

Irritatingly, he was right again. I had forgotten that.

"I could send a pigeon," Lara suggested.

"Would take too long," said Zack. "Brainwaves could take off at any time."

"We could write a note in the wrapper of a Mars bar," said Serge.

"And how would that help?" asked Zack.

"I do not know. But it would mean we were in

possession of a Mars bar." Serge's belly grumbled.

Miss Dunham began jogging on the spot. "I could sneak out of the resort, scale the small peak on the edge of the park, run down the other side and swim across the river until I'm far enough away to get a signal." She threw in a couple of star-jumps. "I'd be back in an hour."

"You'd never make it past the surveillance cameras," said Zack. He was full of objections.

I could tell that Miss Dunham was disappointed at not being able to demonstrate her supreme fitness. I watched her continue to bounce up and down, working off steam. While my brother shot down each fresh idea, I felt a new one poised at the foot of the wall-bars of my mind.

I clicked my fingers. "The solution is obvious. We need to take down the treetop adventure park."

17
HEADS UP!

Billed as a "Thrilling, dizzying treetop adventure", Heads Up! was a combination of zip lines, rope ladders and platforms that formed an obstacle course set high in the forest canopy. More importantly, I had determined it as the most likely location of the jamming device.

As with most of the attractions in the resort, this one was plastered with "Danger – Out of Order" signs. Having no other option, we chose to ignore them.

Lara squinted up at the tallest tree. "There's something attached to the trunk."

"I'm betting that's the electronic jammer," I said confidently. "It stands to reason if you're going to blanket the resort with a signal, you'd put the equipment in the highest spot."

"Can you take it out?" asked Zack.

"A few well-placed squirrels should do the trick," she replied, and patted her hip pocket, where her mobile was tucked inside.

Lara having her phone was a piece of luck. Her mum had confiscated it following the receipt of a shocking bill, which in fact I had run up by making calls in a parallel universe. But following endless pleading and what sounded like a lot of door-slamming, she had returned the phone to her daughter prior to their arrival at Great Minds.

"Once we take care of the jamming signal I can phone out," she said.

"Hang on," said Zack. "Won't Lor-Ayn be suspicious that it's gone down?"

"Unlikely," I said. "Everything in this place is always breaking."

Satisfied that the plan remained sound, Lara used her Dark Flutter animal powers to round up a squad of squirrels and send them scurrying to the top of the tree. The wait was agonising. Knowing that Lor-Ayn could launch Brainwaves at any moment meant there wasn't a second to lose, so we had decided to split forces. While

Lara, Zack and I dealt with the jammer, Miss Dunham had returned to her motorhome to collect equipment for the main assault on Brainwaves. Meanwhile, Serge was scouring the resort for tinfoil, from which to construct Lor-Ayn's prison. I had also asked him to pop back to our caravan to pick up something else essential to the plan.

A few minutes later the squirrels returned. With bad news.

"There are guards." Lara translated the chirping creatures. "My squirrels can't get to the jammer."

"Blazers?" I peered up into the tree canopy, trying to catch sight of them, but the leaves blocked my view.

Lara's squirrels couldn't explain precisely what they'd seen, but whoever it was they weren't Great Minds staff. The best translation Lara could put on their chattering was "bubble-heads".

"Looks like we'll have to do this ourselves," said Zack.

Lara could have called on some birds to fly us quickly up to the top of the tree, but we decided that using a superpower like that risked alerting the guards to our presence. So we did it the old-fashioned way.

I placed a foot on the nearest rope ladder. I had barely begun to climb when the rope gave a creak and snapped, sending me crashing to the ground. I hauled myself back to my feet, muttering, "This thing is a death-trap."

I resumed my climb. I could tell that Zack wanted to take control of my body, since he was far better at this stuff than me. I felt him nudge my fingers and adjust my foot placement in order to ascend more effectively. I didn't object. Under normal circumstances we would be attached to a harness so that in the event of something going wrong, we wouldn't fall messily to our deaths. But even if we could find one, a harness would only have slowed us down. Each section was marked with a sign that indicated the appropriate age range for that level. We passed through ages 7–11, scaling the lower reaches with ease, but as we went higher the difficulty of the obstacles increased. We pushed on, leaving behind a sign that read "Age 12 and above".

I was in unknown territory.

The wooden platforms became narrower and set further apart, meaning we had to take ever greater leaps to continue our progress. It was a bit like playing a video-game – but with only one life. And the higher we climbed the more blustery became the conditions.

I jumped a gap to another platform. Halfway across, the wind caught me and blew me off target. I was sure I was going to miss the platform but then I felt Zack take control. In mid-air he shifted my body position

and angled my feet. I thudded down on the edge of the platform, wobbled, but stayed upright.

"Got you," he said.

I lay down on my back and drew relieved breaths. That had been a close one. Lara crouched next to me and patted my shoulder.

"Come on. Nearly there."

It had taken us fifteen minutes and a near-fatal tumble, but the topmost platform was within sight. Two metres above it, attached to the trunk, was the jamming device we had come to disable.

"Funny," Lara whispered. "I don't see the guards the squirrels were talking a—" She paused. "Wait a minute. *There.*"

A glint of light reflected off what I recognised as a helmet visor. "Bubble-heads," I mumbled, and understood what the squirrels had been on about.

The jammer was guarded by the squad of paintball-gun-wielding space marines we had encountered on arriving at Great Minds. Their camouflaged uniforms had kept them hidden until now. One of them slid back his helmet visor, revealing his face.

It was Josh.

He had the same blank expression I'd seen on the Blazers and I realised that the space marines were under

Lor-Ayn's mind-control. Josh scratched his nose and put the visor back in place.

I was just figuring out how to sneak past when there was a creak from the other end of the platform. It bowed with the weight of a space marine who had just jumped down from the branches. The marine raised his weapon. There was a scrabbling sound above me and the first marine was swiftly joined by the rest of his squad. They surrounded Lara and me from various positions in the trees, their rifles trained on us.

"Luke Parker," said Josh. "Prepare to be atomised!"

It was the same thing he'd said the first time we'd met like this. Big deal. A few paintballs might sting a bit but they were hardly a danger.

"Uh-oh," said Zack. "This is bad."

"What are you talking abou—"

The marines let loose with a fierce barrage. And at that moment I understood why Zack was so concerned. Splat. Splat. Splat. The force of multiple paintball impacts drove me to the edge of the platform. The space marines didn't let up. My foot slipped and my balance went with it. With a cry I dangled over the drop.

"Luke, we're going over!" Zack shouted. "Grab something. Quick!"

I felt myself slip off, and flailed for the platform. I

caught the edge with my fingertips but I wasn't strong enough to hang on.

I fell through the treetops.

I hit a branch and then another, slowing my descent, but then my luck ran out. I continued to fall, plunging uncontrollably to the ground. A serious injury – or worse – awaited me at the bottom. Then suddenly I was aware of the flapping of wings. Dozens of small birds swooped out of the trees and dug their claws into my clothes. They arrested my fall and, straining with all their tiny might, they manoeuvred me back to the relative safety of the treetop platform, dropping me next to Lara.

She narrowed her eyes at the space marines and shouted another series of bird-calls. In seconds the birds had formed a feathery shield around us. Using their flapping wings they generated a powerful wind that deflected the incoming paintballs. I'd never been that impressed with Dark Flutter's creature powers, but this was amazing.

Shielded from the projectiles, she carved a swathe through the space marines' ranks and bore steadily towards the target. However, it remained high out of her reach at the top of the tree. Another call brought more birds to her, clustering around her trainers until they looked like Hermes' winged sandals. She took off, flying over the helmeted heads of the stunned space marines to set down directly in front of the locked cabinet that held the jamming equipment. Crouched there she produced another creature – a brightly coloured centipede – and held it to the keyhole. It wriggled inside, its feet tickling the mechanism like a living lock-pick, and a few seconds later the cabinet was open. Lara swiftly located the controls and flicked the off-switch. The jammer powered down with a whine. Then, for good measure, she snapped off a thick branch and shoved it into the device. There was a crackle, and sparks flew. No one was using that thing again.

Without pausing for breath, Lara gathered me up and in seconds we were flying over the treetops. There was no point worrying about keeping a low profile now. The space marines continued firing their weapons but we were quickly out of range. I started to congratulate Lara, but Zack got in first, praising his fellow superhero. He and I were brothers, but the two of them shared a bond I would never fully appreciate. A few minutes later Lara set us down at the rendezvous point, a bicycle store near the entrance to Brainwaves. We were safely hidden from sight, unless someone decided they wanted to hire a bike.

Serge was already there, putting the finishing touches to the tinfoil prison. He'd fashioned it from a catering

pack and two disposable baking trays. Now he took it apart for ease of carrying. The prison was constructed of six tabbed and slotted pieces. I'd had to abandon my favourite Deadpool backpack in Brainwaves, so I tucked the pieces in my second-favourite – Doctor Strange – ready for rapid assembly when the time came.

"I made these also," he said, passing me three tinfoil hats, one for each member of S.C.A.R.F. (Miss Dunham came with her own.)

I stowed them in the backpack next to the prison and said, "Do you have the phone numbers?"

"*Oui,*" he replied, giving them to me.

Lara pulled out her mobile. "One bar," she said, checking the signal strength. "It's enough."

I turned to her. "Make the first call."

18
OPERATION DOMINO EFFECT

Scattered clouds had swept across the sky for most of the day, but as we observed Brainwaves from our hiding place the sun momentarily broke through, lighting up the grimy glass exterior of the water-park-spaceship. I couldn't help remembering that this was the scene of our failed first mission. Unlike then, we were in no doubt that this time an evil extraterrestrial intelligence lay in wait. Obviously, Miss Dunham had believed that the first time too, but now the rest of us were on board.

Operation Domino Effect was underway. But the pieces wouldn't be in place for at least thirty minutes. In that time the rest of us had to be in position, ready to

take advantage of the planned disruption. Each of us had our part to play.

Miss Dunham returned with the equipment she'd promised: binoculars, walkie-talkies, a stopwatch and those little sachets that you put in your pockets to keep your hands warm. She'd come via Brainwaves, having conducted a quick recce.

"I have good news and bad news," she said.

The good news was that every Blazer on the resort was in there. Having them all together helped our plan to take them out at the same time.

"The bad news is that they've posted guards on the water slide." Our intended way in, through the maintenance hatch as before, had been discovered.

"But that's the only route to the command bridge," said Lara.

"Not the only one," said Miss Dunham. "There is the secure lift outside the Cortex Café."

The first wrinkle in my plan had appeared. "But we can't use it," I reminded her. "We don't know how the lock works."

Serge cleared his throat. "I believe that I do. My backpack, please."

I passed it to him. It clinked as he set it down. "When Miss Dunham explained how Sarah Pelham had strolled right in, it got me thinking. I suspect that what we are dealing with is a lock secured not by a retina scanner, nor a fingerprint, but by a nose-print. It is the unique scent that she is wearing which opens the lift."

Genius! I thought.

"Ridiculous," said Zack.

"Not at all," I insisted. "In comics you come across all kinds of mysterious locks. They can be made from Kryptonite, gorgonzola, the soul of an immortal chicken. You name it. A perfume-print makes perfect sense."

"In your world," my brother muttered.

Serge unzipped his backpack and pulled aside the flaps. It was crammed with little glass bottles.

"Utilising my personal aftershave selection, I will attempt to concoct a scent that mimics exactly the one that Sarah is wearing and so unlocks the lift." He gathered his backpack to leave. Miss Dunham handed him a walkie-talkie. "When I have succeeded, I shall send you the coded signal."

I nodded. "And we'll join you. Good luck, Serge."

"And you, *mes amis*." He tipped a finger to his forehead. "*Bonne chance*."

"Wait," said Lara. "I'll go with you. No harm in having some superhero back-up, right?"

Serge smiled and together they left the bicycle

store, joining the stream of children responding to the tempting message still being broadcast by the public address system. Unlike the Blazers standing guard at the entrance, the children were not under Lor-Ayn's mind-control. I guessed that there were too many even for her to enslave all at once, and that's why she'd needed to tempt them into Brainwaves with prizes. I watched as Serge and Lara slipped past the guards, perfectly concealed among the other children.

"They're in," said Miss Dunham, peering through her binoculars. She lowered them and checked her stopwatch. "Twenty-five minutes until first domino," she said. "Time for me to get in position pool-side."

Miss Dunham was the perfect choice to oversee the evacuation. If anyone had experience of getting unwilling children out of a swimming pool in double-quick time, it was her. She wished us good luck and then, like a ghost in white trainers, she flitted from the bike store and disappeared into the crowd.

No sooner had she departed than my walkie-talkie, which was attached to a loop of my backpack, crackled into life and Serge's voice announced, "We are at the secure elevator. The coast, she is clear. Commencing lock decryption."

I keyed the talk button on my walkie-talkie. "Roger that."

Serge kept up a running commentary as he attempted to open the lift. "I am mixing five mils of *Paco Rabanne Pour Homme* with the same amount of Davidoff *Cool Water.*"

There was a pause as he tried the mixture and then I heard a grunt of frustration.

"Nothing. The lock remains secure. I shall continue on to attempt number two. Ah *oui*, my pretty little security device, you will not keep your secrets from me. I *will* unlock your mysteries."

"Is he talking to the lock?" said Zack.

I nodded. "I believe so."

"*Zut!* Another failure." Serge's disappointed voice trickled out of the walkie-talkie. He muttered to himself, "Of course. *Quel idiot!*" He then gave a self-mocking laugh. "I have been using *eau de toilette* and not *parfum.*"

I keyed my talk button. "Serge, I have no idea what that means."

"It means that I must increase the concentration of the solution," he replied. "But I am confident that I will soon have this lift open. *Red Five, commence your attack run.*"

That was the coded signal. Time for Zack and me

to join the mission. I slung the backpack containing the tinfoil prison across my shoulders and stood up, narrowly avoiding knocking over a unisex 27.5 inch Mountain Bike from the rack.

"Serge has a *lot* of aftershave," said Zack.

"Lucky for us," I said.

As we approached the entrance I saw Blazers on the door. I recognised two of them from the spa. They sported the same blank expressions I'd encountered on every member of mind-controlled staff. I lowered my head and walked among the latest group of children, hoping to pass unnoticed. I was almost past the guards when Serge's voice blared from my walkie-talkie.

"I am now adding my sample-size Calvin Klein *Obsessed* to my Dior *Sauvage*."

Desperately I swatted the volume button and turned him down, but not quickly enough. The guards stared, confused by what they'd heard, and not a little suspicious.

"What was that?" asked one.

"Uh, a podcast?" I said weakly.

I thought they'd bought my explanation and were about to let me past, but I was wrong.

One of them stepped in front of me and said, "What's it called then, this podcast?"

"It's called ... um ... what *is* it called?"

"Close Shave," whispered Zack.

"Brilliant! I mean, it's Close Shave. Because of the ... you get it. It's a series. Kind of a will-he-get-away-with-it-or-not thing. I'm addicted. I'll send you the link."

I felt a firm hand on my shoulder. For a second I thought it was another Blazer, but then I glanced back to see with some surprise that it was in fact Miss Dunham.

"Lor-Ayn has instructed me to deal with this one," she declared.

Ah, the old Miss-Dunham-is-a-baddie-and-I-am-her-captive ploy. A classic ruse I'd seen used with great success in any number of comics and films. But would it work now? I held my breath. A moment later the Blazers stood aside to let us pass, sending us on our way with a cheery cry of, "Have a mind-blowing day!"

"Thanks," I whispered to Miss Dunham. "But what are you doing here? You're supposed to be inside."

"We have a problem," she said.

They were mounting up fast. I felt my clothes stick to me as we entered the overheated pool area.

"See what I mean?" She swept an arm across a scene of chaos. It was child soup. Every cubic centimetre of water contained at least ten kids. The flumes were backed up with even more of them, squirming and shouting. The

noise was deafening.

"I think we've underestimated the numbers," she said.

"No, it's fine," I said, affecting a light tone. But I was hiding my own concern. There were more kids here than at the Pavilion leisure pool on a summer bank holiday. "The plan will work." I crossed my fingers and hoped she wouldn't notice.

"Did you just cross your fingers?" blurted Zack.

Thankfully, at that moment Serge's excited voice burst from my walkie-talkie. "The elevator is unlocked!"

"Good work," I replied.

"*Oui*, the key was Chanel. Naturally."

There was a hiss of static and a clatter, as if someone else had grabbed the walkie-talkie, and then Lara cut in. "He's amazing," she said proudly. "And he smells sensational."

Miss Dunham checked her stopwatch. "Fifteen minutes until kick-off."

I got back to Serge, informing him that Zack and I would be right with him. As planned, Miss Dunham stayed behind at the pool-side to oversee the evacuation. I set off through the press of people and had almost reached the corridor when I felt myself come to a sudden and unexpected halt.

With growing panic I tried to lift one foot and then

the other, but I couldn't move a muscle. The heat and the humidity were overwhelming. I felt myself weaken. There was little doubt in my mind – Lor-Ayn had taken control of me.

19
NEVER TOUCH A GLOWING PLINTH

My panic lasted all of three seconds, and then the crowd of children thinned and I saw the true reason for the emergency stop.

Cara Lee.

She lay on a sunlounger on the fake beach, wearing sunglasses, reading a magazine and sipping a drink through a curly straw. My brother must have spotted her and slammed on the brakes. I knew that Cara was in terrible danger being here. But I knew too that she was perfectly capable of looking after herself. Still, I felt an urge to protect her and hold her and kiss her and—

Whoa!

"Zack, please keep those thoughts to yourself."

"Sorry." He cleared his throat.

"OK, let's go." I tried to move but my feet wouldn't budge. "Zack, the plan is to get to the command bridge before this thing takes off. What are you doing?"

I could feel him gazing at Cara through my eyes.

"I'm supposed to meet her here, remember?" He sounded alarmed. "If I don't show, she'll think I've stood her up. She'll never ask me on a date ever again."

Oh, for goodness' sake. Now, as with every other moment in life, was not the time to be worrying about things like girls. "Small problem with that," I reminded him. "*Zack* is supposed to meet her."

"I *am* Zack," he protested.

Around Cara he frequently forgot his own name. This time he'd forgotten his own body. I reminded him of his predicament.

"Then you have to talk to her," he said. "Tell her why I couldn't make it."

"You mean because of the mind-swap, the body-share and the evil brain-in-a-jar?"

"NO!" he blurted. "Do not under any circumstances mention any of that stuff. She'll think I'm weird."

"So what do I tell her?"

"I don't know." He threw up my hands. "You'll think

of something." And then he added, "Just don't be a dork."

I should've been on my way to the rendezvous with the others, but I calculated that I would waste more time arguing with my brother than agreeing to his demand. I stepped on to the fake beach and made my way over to Cara. Unlike every other kid in the place, she didn't seem interested in winning prizes. She appeared to be much more concerned about finding just the right spot beneath the artificial lights. I stopped in front of her recliner, my shadow falling across her lounging body. She lowered her sunglasses and peered over them at me.

"Kid, you're in my light."

I shuffled to one side. I still wasn't sure what to tell her. Zack had ruled out all of the reasonable explanations.

"You OK?" she said. "You look kind of—"

"Zack's dead."

I heard Zack groan.

Cara sat up and whipped off her sunglasses. "What?!"

"Not dead. I meant … playing minigolf." It was an OK lie, but not a great one and I felt the need to enhance it. Over the years I'd discovered that the trick to creating a really convincing lie was to add detail. It's called embellishing. "Yeah, he's playing a round with Tabitha Owen."

In my head I could hear weeping.

"I'm so glad he found something better to do," said Cara.

It was weird. Her words said that she was pleased, but her voice suggested the opposite.

She gave a bored sigh. "So why are you telling me this?"

"Because he didn't want you to think he'd stood you up."

My right leg kicked my left ankle.

"Ow!"

I felt Zack take control of both legs and rapidly propel me away from Cara's side. She popped her sunglasses back on, unfolded her magazine with a snap and stretched out again on the sunlounger.

"Hey! I wasn't finished," I complained. "I was going to warn her about Lor-Ayn. What are you doing?"

"Getting you out of here before you do any more damage."

Damage? "I thought that went very well."

"What was I thinking? Oh god…"

With Zack making small moaning noises, I left the pool area and headed into the long, brightly lit corridor that formed the outer rim of the water park. As I traced the curving passageway I felt the floor beneath my feet

vibrate to the thrum of distant machinery. Now that I knew the true nature of the place, the mechanical noise took on a new significance. Deep within the building, interplanetary engines ramped up, preparing to launch the water park into space. It was the first time that I'd thought about the layout of Brainwaves. It had been designed as a series of concentric circles (concentric means a bunch of circles with the same centre and was not, as Lara claimed, a trick to help you concentrate). And at the heart of the structure brooded an alien queen.

The passageway was busy with contractors carrying out what had to be launch preparations. One mind-controlled electrician put the finishing touches to a complicated section of wiring, another crouched at an unshielded computer station soldering components, and several Blazers performed what could only be final inspections. All worked in eerie silence. There was no way to sneak around them. I'd just have to hope that my theory about Lor-Ayn was correct. I began to thread my way past, my head fixed forward to avoid eye contact.

No one gave me a second look.

They had no other choice. Lor-Ayn had given them one task and one only. They weren't allowed to take any initiative. Make any decisions of their own. It was like the national curriculum but with mind-control.

I smiled to myself. Lor-Ayn's grip on her mind-slaves would be her downfall.

Deeper and deeper I went, passing through each ring of the circular structure, heading for the centre.

"I wonder how she's powering this thing," I said. "Warp Drive, Hyperdrive, Infinite Improbability Drive?"

"I don't care if it's Google Drive," Zack snapped. "So long as my body isn't a passenger when she takes off."

My destination lay just around the next bend. I ignored the entrance to the Cortex Café and shuffled to the, well, not the corner because it was a curve.

"Zack, what do you call the corner of a curve?"

"*Now* you want to start revising?"

Before me lay the express lift to the command bridge. I couldn't see Serge or Lara and was about to raise the walkie-talkie to contact them when I saw a shadow fall against the opposite wall. A second later Lor-Ayn came around the bend. She hovered a metre or so off the floor, presumably held aloft by her own mind-powers. Her Bluetooth speaker was stuck to the base of her jar with packing tape. She was accompanied by Sarah Pelham and a handful of elite Blazer guards (I knew they were elite because the piping on their blazers was gold, not the usual silver). Quickly, I retraced my steps and ducked

into the café. I held my breath and eavesdropped on their conversation as they glided past.

"Preparations are on schedule, Your Majesty," said Sarah. "We will be ready to launch within the hour."

It was significant news but Lor-Ayn didn't seem to notice. "Have you seen the electrician's bill? It's criminal. Good thing I plan to be in another galaxy before it's due. I'd like to see him chase that payment." She gave a cruel laugh. "Now, let me inspect the fuel status."

The two of them disappeared round the bend of the corridor. As their conversation faded, I heard the sound of the lift doors opening behind me. I turned to see Serge and Lara inside. They beckoned to me urgently and, pausing only to check for more Blazer patrols, I left my concealment and joined them.

"Lor-Ayn's checking the fuel tanks or something. Now's our chance." I slapped the button for the basement and with a jolt our descent began. By the time Lor-Ayn returned to the command bridge, we would be in position. It was all going surprisingly well. As the lift continued its descent I recalled that the last time we were here our plan had fallen apart around us. In fact, during my time as commander of S.C.A.R.F. I'd yet to hatch a plan that went smoothly. That would be another chapter in my guide – "Plan For Your Plan Not To Go

As Planned". I hoped that this would be the day it all ran like clockwork, but a little voice in my head told me to be prepared for the worst.

"Was that your little voice?" I asked Zack.

"No."

"Just checking."

I reached into my backpack. "OK," I said, passing out the tinfoil hats that Serge had made along with the prison. "Headgear. On."

"But Lor-Ayn's not on the bridge," Zack objected.

"And I'm not taking any chances," I said.

Zack prodded our hat and complained. "I feel like a human burrito."

"Better that than having your mind hijacked," I pointed out.

"Mmm, burritos," said Serge with a distant look.

The lift came to a juddering stop, the doors opened and we were presented with a view of the command bridge. Blazers moved silently from one computer station to another, presumably running pre-flight diagnostics, checking the oil was topped up, that kind of thing. Like their counterparts in the corridors above, they paid no attention to us, fixed as they were on their individual tasks with single-minded focus.

They streamed around the glass containment tube

that held Zack's body.

Someone had put him in his Star Lad costume, but even through his mask I could see that his eyes were dull, his jaw slack – nobody was home.

"Find the controls for the tube," Zack said. "We have to get me out of there."

"And we're looking for anything that might be a communication device," I added. "We have to contact Lor-Ayn's homeworld."

As we combed the various control panels I couldn't help noticing that at the centre of the room stood the now unoccupied plinth on which Lor-Ayn's jar had rested for a decade. The spinning lights that once formed her impregnable prison were gone, broken apart by Star Lad's hijacked superpowers.

The plinth was bleeping. The sound repeated on a loop.

"Got it!" cried Lara, standing over a slider control.

There was a whoosh as the tube retracted into the ceiling. Zack's body was free. However, it remained where it stood, unmoving. Without Zack's consciousness inside, it was as useful as a squeezy bottle without the ketchup.

"Wait *un* moment. Look at this." Serge stood in front of Lor-Ayn's plinth. The surface pulsed with a purple light, keeping perfect time with the repetitive bleeping. "What do you suppose it is?"

"This used to be a prison," said Lara. "Maybe it's an alarm."

"Yeah, linked directly to Space Police HQ." I reached out to touch the light. Immediately, Zack took control of my body and yanked the arm back.

"What d'you think you're doing?! After all the world-ending hassle we've been through? You never touch random glowing plinths."

The alarm fell silent and the light dimmed.

"I didn't do anything!" I protested.

"Native lifeforms detected," announced a weird, disembodied voice. "Prepare for incoming transmission."

20
WE DON'T NEED NO THOUGHT CONTROL

A new sound arose from the plinth. This one was musical, like a flourish of trumpets. As the last note faded an image appeared: a holographic projection of three brains in jars. Unlike Lor-Ayn's simple container, each was a masterpiece of the jar-maker's art. And each occupied a little throne. The jar on the left seemed to be held in the talons of a dragon-like creature sculpted from silver and emeralds; the one in the middle dripped with golden leaves and was topped with an elaborate gem-studded crown; while the third sported what looked like headlamps and a paint-job that made it look surprisingly like a Ford Focus with go-faster stripes. The crowned jar flickered with multicoloured light and a sweet-natured voice began to speak.

"Greetings, Earthlings, permit me to introduce myself. I am Queen Mee-Grayn the First, of the Cerebran royal family. I have the regrettable distinction of being sister to Lor-Ayn the Unspeakable, Bringer of Pain, Smiter of Jars, Arch-enemy of the Cerebrans." The other two brains gurgled nervously. "Our subspace sensors, which monitor her prison, indicate that the force field confining her has been breached and she has escaped." Her jar trembled and the crown clinked against the glass. "I have dreaded the coming of this day. But fear not – precautions have been taken. As she is the most dangerous and vicious criminal in our history, we have put in place measures to ensure that peace and happiness prevail. An automatic containment system has been activated."

For once someone else had done the hard work. Lor-Ayn's own people had outsmarted her.

The holographic image changed to show an image of Earth from space. "The containment system has been cloaked in your planet's orbit since the day Lor-Ayn's sentence commenced." There was a ripple in space as alien stealth technology adjusted to reveal a series of warheads glowing in the sunlit vacuum of space.

"Twelve of our most advanced Muclear missiles," explained Mee-Grayn. It was a weapons platform. "They have been precisely calibrated to reduce your planet to dust, thus eliminating any possibility that my sister might escape and return to our world."

"Are you kidding?!" Zack's exclamation brought the queen's speech to a temporary halt. "What about peace and happiness?"

The alien-cloaking technology reactivated, hiding the weapons. The image of Mee-Grayn and the rest of the royal family returned to the screen.

"Oh, you thought I meant Earth? Yes, I see how the phrasing might have been ambiguous. Please accept my sincere apologies."

"So you'll stand down the Muclear missiles?" I said.

The queen's laugh was like a tinkle of bells but her voice was gruff. "Not a chance. Lor-Ayn is *really* dangerous. I mean, would *you* lock your sister up in a prison halfway across the galaxy if she wasn't the most vile, vindictive being in the universe?"

Even so, it seemed like overkill to me. "To put a stop to one bad brain, you're willing to wipe out all life on Earth?"

There was another pause as she considered my question. "Yes."

I don't know what she said right after that, because her words were drowned out by our howls of outrage.

"No point in delaying the inevitable," said Mee-Grayn. "Launching missiles in five … four…"

She continued to count down. Somewhere in orbit, alien guidance systems were waking up and targeting computers were drawing a bullseye on Earth. And there was nothing we could do to stop them.

"One!"

I braced myself. Right now rocket engines were firing, missiles were leaping from their rails. At least, that's what I assumed was happening, but when after a few seconds Mee-Grayn piped up again, it was clear something had gone wrong.

"What do you mean, it's jammed?" she responded to some distant missile-command operator. "Well, when was it last serviced?" She sighed. "Fine. Send an engineer to Earth immediately. No, I do not have the number. You know what, don't bother. I'll go myself." She switched her attention to us. "Earthlings, it seems you have a reprieve. It will take some time for me to cross the vast interstellar gulf between our worlds. And that's assuming I can get a weapons engineer on an emergency call-out." I could tell that she was working out her timings. She hummed and hawed. "I estimate my arrival in ten million neural

cycles. On your Earth scale, about three quarters of an hour."

It wasn't long, but at least the Cerebrans' poor maintenance schedule had offered us a sliver of hope. "Queen Mee-Grayn," I said. "If we can recapture your sister before you get here, will you call off the missile launch?"

Mee-Grayn's answer came in the form of a mocking laugh. "Recapture the most lethal being ever to occupy a jar? I wish you good luck with that." The colour of the liquid in her jar turned from clear to red. "You're going to need it."

With that, the transmission ended, and she and the rest of the Cerebran royal family vanished.

"Oooh, I hate her!" screeched a voice from behind us. We whirled round to find Lor-Ayn floating at the entrance to the command bridge. "And did you see that crown? That's *mine*. Doesn't even fit her stupid little jar."

As she poured out a series of hurtful comments about her sister, Zack muttered to me, "And you were going to help free *this*?"

"She said she was a princess in distress. She seemed very plausible."

"Course she did. I mean, if you can't trust an alien

brain-in-a-jar with a galactic criminal record, who can you trust?"

I think he was being sarcastic, but I ignored him as an idea had occurred to me. Zack and I had fallen out loads over the years. We could get seriously angry with each other, but nothing had ever come between us that was unforgiveable. I took advantage of a pause in Lor-Ayn's tirade to speak up.

"Why don't you talk to her?" I said. "I'm sure if we opened a hailing frequency or whatever, we could get her back and the two of you could sort this out. Sister-to-sister."

Lor-Ayn's jar swivelled a hundred and eighty degrees.

"I think she just turned her back on us," said Lara.

"I'm not talking to *her*," Lor-Ayn pouted.

I shook my hands in frustration. "But then you'll be blown up along with the rest of us."

Lor-Ayn's jar whirled back around. "I anticipated my sister's clumsy strategy – you never get more than a three-year warranty on Muclear missiles. Everyone knows that. I will be far from Earth by the time she arrives to launch them. The fate of a few billion hairless monkeys is of no concern to me."

The clock ticked towards the crucial second when Operation Domino Effect would – well, take effect. But

it was still a few tantalising minutes away. Right now, we had one chance – the tinfoil prison in my backpack. If we kept her talking long enough maybe I could get to the pieces and assemble the box.

"What are you going to do with us?" I asked.

"You will join the rest of the children in the pool area for an afternoon of entertaining water-based activities."

I wasn't falling for that one. "We know it's not a dodgy water park," I said. "It's a spaceship *disguised* as a dodgy water park."

Lor-Ayn's voice turned brittle. "It's an all-action, fun-for-the-family, adrenalin-filled epic-day-out water park."

"The wave machine's broken," I informed her.

"It's on the list," she said tightly.

"I do not comprehend," said Serge. "Why would you wish to take so many children with you?"

"Sparky little numbers," she said.

It was the same phrase she'd used before and as she said it the answer to Serge's question leapt out at me like a monster from a wardrobe. Among the list of criteria for her Star Lad candidates I remembered: "*Wattage*."

Serge gasped with understanding.

"Your ship's power source is human minds," I said. "*Children's*."

"Very good, Luke. Or did Zack figure it out? He's the clever one, isn't he?"

I smarted with resentment.

"When my ship launches, its hemispheric engines will suck the energy from the brain of every child in the water park. I have just inspected my fuel supply and, as you can see, I am almost ready to depart."

The view-screen displayed an image of the main pool, where hundreds of children played and splashed, unaware that they were about to be drained like a value pack of double-A batteries on Christmas morning.

"And now you three bright sparks will join the rest," Lor-Ayn gloated.

I clasped my tinfoil hat. "You can't force us."

"Yes, your aluminium-based food-wrapping product presents a problem for me. But not for them."

Lor-Ayn didn't need to control our minds when she had the Blazers. She commanded them to surround us. They closed in, whipping the protective hats from our heads, balling them up and depositing them in the nearest waste basket. Then each took an arm and we were manhandled towards the lift.

We passed Zack's body, standing there like an empty suit of Iron Man armour. All the power we needed to defeat Lor-Ayn was stored inside it, ready to be activated,

if only Zack could reach out and zip himself up inside. I half expected my brother to pull off a last-ditch rescue; to save the day with seconds to spare. But then there was a whiff of perfume and the lift doors opened. We were bundled inside.

Just as the doors slid shut on the bridge, there was a bleep from Lara's phone. Her alarm sounded. It was now exactly thirty minutes since she'd made the first call of Operation Domino Effect.

This game wasn't over yet.

With Lor-Ayn's laughter ringing in our ears, we were taken to our fate. The Blazers marched us along the corridor until we were back at the main pool. I searched the crowd for Miss Dunham. With a bit of luck she'd figure out that we were in a tight spot and come to our aid. But I couldn't see her anywhere.

She wasn't the only one missing. I noticed that the Blazers who'd been guarding the pool area had all left their posts. And then, above the clamour of squealing children, I tuned in to an unmistakable puttering sound from just outside. The noise reached our captors' ears and I sensed confusion – and horrified recognition – among them. I seized my chance. Wrenching my arm free, I broke away and bolted for the door.

Pizza delivery bikes, row upon row of them, straggled

across the entrance. I cast a satisfied eye along the ranks of mopeds and scooters. It looked like every takeaway delivery bike for miles around was in Great Minds. The mind-controlled Blazers were attempting to fend off a tide of helmeted riders, receipts in hand, all loudly trying to figure out who had ordered two hundred pepperoni pizzas (and fifty veggie supremes) but, more urgently, who was going to pay for them.

I smiled at the scene of organised chaos. Josh had given me the idea. On the first day he'd told me that the takeaway deliveries used to drive the Blazers bonkers. Earlier, I had sent Serge to fetch all the menus from our caravan. That gave us the phone numbers. Then, with the jamming signal down, Lara had made the calls. Operation Domino Effect was go!

As planned, Lor-Ayn was forced to use every one of her mind-slaves to deal with the horde of disgruntled delivery riders. She was stretched to breaking point. Now to push her over.

"FREE PIZZA! OUTSIDE NOW!"

I stood on the edge of the pool and shouted the words. I hadn't counted on the noise level and for a moment feared I'd been drowned out, but the kids nearest me must have heard, as the message spread through the crowd like norovirus in a ball-pit.

There was a brief moment of silence, broken only by the lapping of waves. Then a cheer went up that tingled to the ceiling of Brainwaves. The water churned as hungry swimmers clambered out of the pool and stampeded through the door. The pizza wasn't free, of course, but the lie would get them to safety – and remove Lor-Ayn's fuel source. She wasn't going anywhere.

A scattering of swimmers remained in the water.

"Why do they not depart like the rest?" asked Serge.

"Gluten-free," I replied.

Suddenly Lara pointed all the way across the main pool. "Incoming!" she cried.

On the far side, hovering a metre or two above the water, was Lor-Ayn. She took an erratic course, weaving from side to side like an airliner in turbulence, but even with her unsteady approach her destination was clear.

"She is heading straight for us!" said Serge.

I knew what I had to do. And fast. Unhooking my backpack, I emptied its contents on to the floor. I surveyed the six tabbed pieces of the home-made tinfoil prison shining under the lights.

"OK, here goes." I picked up two of the pieces. "Insert tab A into slot B."

"Quickly, Luke," said Lara.

Lor-Ayn's flightpath dipped and she skimmed across the pool, low enough to send up a bow wave. She was like a fin in the water. The few remaining swimmers screamed and scrambled out of her path. She drew ever closer, her Bluetooth speaker dangling. Judging by what she was saying, her brain was here but her attention was focused outside.

"For the last time I did not order two hundred pepperoni pizzas," she raged. "No, I don't know who's going to pay for them. What do you mean, where's your tip?"

"Hurry up!" urged Zack.

I had completed five of the six sides of the prison, but as I reached for the last piece I saw to my horror that it wasn't there. I grabbed my backpack, upended it and shook out the remaining contents. Out fell a packet of Haribo sours and an old apple core, but no foil side. Without it the prison was incomplete. And useless.

"Luke?" Zack could sense my fear.

"I don't have it!" I yelled.

Lor-Ayn was almost upon us. "You did this!" She switched her attention from the pizza fiasco to us. "I don't know how, but you're responsible. No matter. You cannot stand in my way. I am Lor-Ayn the Unspeakable, Bringer of Pain, Smiter of Jars, Arch-enemy of the

Cerebrans." She reared out of the pool, water streaming off her jar. "Prepare to be *smashed to pieces*."

Perhaps she wasn't as vulnerable as I'd figured. As I looked up at her seemingly unstoppable presence, my attention was split by a still figure standing atop the Cerebral Aqueduct.

It was Miss Dunham.

If my eyes didn't deceive me, in each hand she clutched a roll of tinfoil. Taking a short run-up, she leapt from the slide with a furious cry, brandishing the tinfoil before her like Wolverine's adamantium claws. Her gym teacher timing was perfect. She intercepted Lor-Ayn at the uppermost point of her trajectory, thudding down with both feet on top of the jar, her knees bending to absorb the impact.

Like a fat fly stunned by a surprise swat, Lor-Ayn reeled beneath the unexpected assault and quickly lost height. Miss Dunham sat astride the jar, clinging on with her thighs, leaving her hands free to unspool the foil. Riding the bucking brain, she wrapped one roll around the jar in a continuous length, then did the same with the second. With Lor-Ayn swaddled to her satisfaction she discarded the cardboard inner tubes like a couple of expended booster rockets.

The effect was instant. Without her mind-power to

keep her aloft, Lor-Ayn's jar dropped out of the air. Miss Dunham rode it all the way down to the poolside, leaping off at the last second to land with a controlled forward roll. The jar smacked against the tiles but didn't shatter. Instead it bounced a couple of times and trundled to a stop at my feet.

Lara, Serge and I looked in stunned amazement at Miss Dunham, who was already brushing herself off and striding in our direction.

Lor-Ayn's voice stabbed out of the muffled Bluetooth speaker.

"You can't do this to me!" she ranted. "I am a princess! I am the rightful heir to the Cerebran throne! I will destroy you! I will—"

I felt through the tinfoil for the speaker's power button and, with a flick of the switch, cut her off mid-flow. Miss Dunham's foil wrap had effectively blocked Lor-Ayn's mind-powers but I wanted to make doubly sure she couldn't escape. I rechecked my backpack, to discover the missing side of foil jammed against the lining.

Miss Dunham bent down, wrapped her arms around the jar and heaved it through the open top of my tinfoil Arkham Asylum.

"Insert tab E into slot F." I slid the last pieces together, fixed the lid in place and sealed her up inside. Lor-Ayn

was back where she belonged, behind bars. Or, at least, behind Bacofoil.

It took me a moment to realise what we had accomplished. Operation Domino Effect was a total success.

It was over. We'd won.

21
I CAN SEE CLEARLY NOW LOR-AYN HAS GONE

The victory party would come later. Probably a big get-together in the pool with all those pizzas, if we could persuade the delivery riders to leave them behind.

"Luke, get your head in the game." Zack's urgent voice punctured my daydream. "This is not over."

I slid the imprisoned Lor-Ayn into my backpack for ease of transport, slung it over my back and tightened the chest straps.

Lor-Ayn was out of action but we still had a job to do. Lara, Serge, Miss Dunham and I set off back through Brainwaves, heading for the command bridge. As we followed the long curve of the outer corridor, we filled

Miss Dunham in on Mee-Grayn and the missiles.

She grimaced. "They're going to muke us from orbit."

I sprinted to keep up with the others, feeling the weight of the captured brain in my backpack bouncing against my shoulders. I studied Miss Dunham carefully. I could tell that Zack's opinion of her had swung right around. At first he had dismissed her seemingly nutty ideas on the basis that she was as unhinged as a door that our dad's tried to fit. But she'd been right about a lot of things, and following her heroic leap off the water slide and subsequent ninja take-down of Lor-Ayn, we were in her debt. I marvelled at the transformation. And I was jealous too. It didn't seem to matter what I did, I would always just be Zack's little brother.

It wasn't long before we found ourselves outside the perfume-print-secured lift.

Sarah Pelham stood in our way. The jacket of her Great Minds uniform had fallen open and several buttons were missing. It looked like they'd been ripped off in anger.

"Don't try to stop us," I said.

Sarah shook her head. "I'm me again. I want to help." Released from years spent serving Lor-Ayn, she craved something else too. "And my name isn't Sarah. That's what *she* named me." Her face glowed with her new-found freedom. This was a significant moment: the first time she had reclaimed her identity since Lor-Ayn took it away from her. "My name is Saoirse."

I must have misheard. "Sorry, did you say *Sher Sa*?"

She sounded it out again, slowly.

"OK, yes, I've got it," said Lara. "*Say Oarsh A*."

"Almost. Try again," said Sarah. "It's—"

I raised a finger. "Would it be all right if we carried on calling you Sarah, just for now? It's only, with everything else that's going on…"

She tutted and folded her arms. "Fine."

The bridge was empty of crew. No longer subject to Lor-Ayn's power, the Blazers had fled. Even her elite guard had ditched her at the first opportunity. I couldn't help wondering that if she'd taken a different approach then maybe they would have been more loyal. For instance, if she'd operated a clearly defined career path with pay and bonuses, rather than enslaving them, they might have hung about. It was too late for Lor-Ayn, and it might be for us too, if we couldn't contact her sister. Assuming Mee-Grayn was on schedule, it would be another fifteen minutes before she arrived in Earth orbit and her engineer could begin working on the missiles. At least that gave us some breathing space.

"We have to re-establish contact with the Cerebrans," said Zack. "So let's figure out how this communication

plinth thing works."

"I can help with that," said Sarah. "As well as being a resort host I was meant to pilot the ship. Lor-Ayn made sure that I have a first-aid badge, a health and safety certificate and an advanced astro-navigation degree. Let me show you the comms panel."

But before she could do that the familiar computer-generated voice filled the bridge. "Prepare for incoming transmission."

What was going on? Surely Mee-Grayn was still deep in hyperspace without a signal? We gathered round the plinth as her image appeared once again in holographic form.

"Earthlings, I am in orbit around your Earth aboard my personal flagship," she said delightedly.

She was early. This was bad.

"Yes, there's usually terrible traffic around this time at Wormhole EM25, but wouldn't you know it – straight through! Must be my lucky day."

Less so for us, I thought to myself. Nonetheless, we were in a very different position from when we'd last spoken. "We did it, Your Majesty," I said, excitedly unzipping her sister from inside my backpack and setting her down on the plinth next to Mee-Grayn. Even though she was safely separated from Lor-Ayn, she shuddered at the sight of her jar.

"Yes, our sensors detected her recapture," she said warily, "but I had to see it with my own occipital lobe."

"She's going nowhere," I said. "You don't have to fire the missiles."

"You have done well, humans," said Mee-Grayn. "Many Cerebran warriors fell in battle attempting to best my terrible sister, but you defeated her in less time than it takes a pituitary gland to secrete a stress hormone. What a remarkable species. I wish we had more time to come to understand one another."

"No problem," I said. "Zack's got a Spanish exchange next term. We could do something like that? But in the meantime can you collect your sister and take her back to a proper prison? Because I don't think our baking tray solution is long-term."

"Good news," she announced. "I have the weapons engineer's report."

What did that have to do with picking up Lor-Ayn?

"It seems the problem was merely a missed software update. Once it's installed and the system reboots, the missile strike will proceed as planned. In … twenty of your Earth minutes."

Miss Dunham's knuckles whitened as she balled her hands into fists. "You double-crossing little—"

"It is an outrage!" cried Serge.

"Typical brain-in-a-jar stab-in-the-back," said Sarah.

"Please," Zack implored her. "Lor-Ayn isn't a threat to anyone. Don't do this."

"Your Highness," said Lara. "She's your responsibility now. Collect your sister and take her home."

I nodded. "Yeah, it's not like she's going to escape into the ventilation ducts, bump off the crew one by one in an increasingly grisly fashion, before blowing you out of an airlock."

"Luke," hissed Zack.

Mee-Grayn laughed. "Take my sister home? Are you pulling my motor cortex? What I will do is commend you on your bravery in recapturing her. Your fleshy bodies will be incinerated in the coming inferno, but know that your names will go down in Cerebran history: Serge, Lara, Miss Dunham and Zuke."

Oh, come on!

Sarah raised a hand. "And Saoirse."

"Hmm," said Mee-Grayn. "You're going to have to spell that."

As much as I wanted to protest the name mishap, there were more pressing things to worry about. I fumbled for the Bluetooth speaker controls on Lor-Ayn's jar.

"No, do not—" Mee-Grayn protested, but she was

too late.

I switched it back on. "I know you two are not exactly friends right now but, Queen Mee-Grayn, if you blow up the earth you'll lose your only sister."

At first, neither sister said anything. Maybe they were sizing each other up. It had been a long time since they spoke. The silence turned out to be the lull before the brainstorm.

"You just don't get it, do you, Luke?" said Lor-Ayn. "Getting rid of me is all she's ever wanted."

"Can you blame me?" snapped Mee-Grayn. "You hated me from the day Mother and Father brought me home from the birthing pods. You've been in a foul mood ever since."

"You try being the big sister," griped Lor-Ayn. "There's a lot of expectation."

"Oh, please, you were the heir. The favoured child."

"Well, you were the pretty one."

"When your friends came round to the palace, you never let me join in your games."

"You always seemed to prefer playing on your own. You turned inwards."

"And you acted out. Used your mind-powers to hurt others."

I had hoped for some sort of ceasefire, but instead the

sisters were growing angrier with one another. And as they hurled their insults, our chances of calling off the missile strike shrank. I had to try something.

"What if Lor-Ayn apologises – would that help?"

"I suppose it might," Mee-Grayn mumbled.

I turned to Lor-Ayn. "Will you say sorry?"

"I will," she said, much to my astonishment. "But only if she says it first."

Mee-Grayn's voice hardened. "It's always about you, isn't it? You have to be the centre of the universe. Mother and Father seemed to think so too. When I was nine they gave away my pet Fluvav because you were allergic to its fur."

"No, no, you've got that all wrong," said Lor-Ayn. "Sister, they lied to you."

"They did?"

I noted the surprise in Mee-Grayn 's voice. Perhaps we were getting somewhere. For Zack and me, some of our closest times as brothers had occurred when we were able to unite against our parents' terrible decisions. Could this be the moment to bring these two together and save the planet?

"They didn't give away your precious Fluvav," said Lor-Ayn evenly. "I poisoned it."

Probably not.

For Mee-Grayn, that was the final straw. If I thought they'd been hard on each other so far, it had nothing on what came next. Insult after insult, slight upon slight, they dredged up every supposed injustice, picked every bone. There was no getting around it: these two hated each other. Until then the possibility had never entered my mind that siblings could fall out and never get back together. It hadn't happened to Zack and me. It wouldn't. But the universe felt like a colder place than I'd believed it to be a minute ago.

There was a final angry exchange involving an accusation from one sister that the other had borrowed her leopard-print jar (or something) without asking, and then Mee-Grayn's image vanished. The conversation was well and truly over.

Lor-Ayn continued to grumble until Sarah switched off her speaker. I could see her take pleasure in the little act. For the first time in years, she was the one in control.

In the silence that followed all I could hear was the tick of the stopwatch. Miss Dunham glanced at the face.

"Fifteen minutes to missile launch."

22
AMALGAMATED FROZEN PEAS

"Maybe *we* can't do anything about those missiles," said Lara, scrolling through her phone. "But I know someone who can." She tapped the contact number and dialled out.

"Amalgamated Frozen Peas," answered a woman's voice.

Serge and I exchanged puzzled looks. I was sure that Lara had misdialled but she didn't even blink.

"Commence unique identification procedure," she instructed. "Delta Niner Squirrel Tango Badger Hedgehog. Authenticate."

"ID authenticated. Putting you through to Star Squad

central operations, Dark Flutter."

In seconds Lara was on the line with Colonel Crowe and a round-table of Star Squad experts, explaining to them the imminent threat from the Cerebran missile battery.

"I have alerted Star Squad Seven," said the colonel. "They are responsible for covering Devon, Cornwall and the parts of Somerset along the M5 corridor. A quick-reaction task force will be at your location in approximately four minutes."

"What about the missiles?" said Lara. "Can you shoot them down before they launch?"

"Star Lad's the boy for that job," said Colonel Crowe. "He can fly up there, detect the missiles and blast them with his telekinetic power. What's his sitrep?"

A sitrep was a situation report.

"Uh, he's temporarily out of action, I'm afraid."

Colonel Crowe absorbed this unwelcome information. "Any chance he'll return at the last minute and save the day?"

Lara glanced at me with a questioning look. Zack grumbled something about pigs flying and snowballs in volcanoes. She returned to the phone.

"I think we have to assume we're on our own, Colonel."

On hearing this, Colonel Crowe sprang into action.

He issued an order to task a high-performance Tracking and Imaging radar system to locate the orbital missile platform. Once they had its coordinates, he informed us, they'd launch Earth's own ground-based missiles in an attempt to shoot it down.

It was worth a try but I doubted it would succeed. From what I'd seen – or rather *not* seen – the Cerebrans had camouflaged their missile platform using advanced alien stealth technology, making it highly unlikely that any Earth radar could detect it. After all, the weapon had been up there for more than a decade. In that time thousands of radars and telescopes had been pointed into orbit, the International Space Station had probably whizzed right by it, and no one had noticed it yet.

I didn't say any of that to my friends. What was the point? I looked around the room. Lara and Serge held hands. Together we'd faced the end of the world four times. Today would make number five. Each time I'd walked to the brink I'd peered over it alongside them – and my brother. As ever, Zack and I were in this together, but sadly this time we were stuck in my powerless body and not his superpowered one. Colonel Crowe was right – we needed Star Lad. But the empty shell stood on the other side of the plinth, about as useful as a sock puppet.

Unless.

Before anyone could argue I'd flicked on Lor-Ayn's speaker. "You moved my mind out of Zack's body. You can move his back into it."

Silence. Either she was still smarting from the tête-à-tête with her sister and wasn't in the mood to talk, or the speaker needed recharging. It slouched into life with a buzz and crackle.

"Release me from my prison and I will help you."

"No way!" Miss Dunham put herself between me and Lor-Ayn. "It's a trick."

"She's right," said Sarah. "The second you let her out of there, she'll use her power against us."

I threw a question out to Star Squad. "Colonel, what are the chances of you destroying those missiles?"

"Who is this? Identify yourself."

He didn't recognise my voice, due to the fact that the only time we'd met I'd been in Zack's body.

"S.C.A.R.F. leader," I replied.

"Who?"

I sighed. "Star Lad's little brother."

His voice brightened. "Ah, the one who missed out on superpowers when he went for a—"

"Yes," I cut him off. "That one. Now, answer my question. What are the odds?"

"Hard to say with any accuracy, but I'd estimate it at

three thousand seven hundred and twenty to one."

I gazed up at Miss Dunham. "Star Lad is our only hope, and Lor-Ayn our only chance of getting him in the air."

"I just don't trust that brain," said Miss Dunham.

"Then use yours, gym teacher!" Lor-Ayn fired back. "Why would I trick you now? As you have observed, I am a creature motivated purely by self-interest. When those missiles strike Earth, I will be destroyed along with the rest of you."

I could see Miss Dunham weighing up her options. On the one hand, Lor-Ayn wasn't going to let herself be wiped out. On the other, evil brain-in-a-jar.

Grudgingly, she stood aside. "OK, but one thing first." She retrieved the crumpled tinfoil hats from the wastepaper basket and passed them out to Lara and Serge. She came to me last.

"I can't," I said. "I need to give her free access to my mind."

She offered the tinfoil protector to Sarah instead. I waited until they'd each fixed their protective headgear, then unwrapped Lor-Ayn, peeling away the layers of foil.

No sooner had the protective cover gone when flashes of light appeared inside the jar, bursting like tiny suns.

She was building up to something, no question. After the sun came forks of hot lightning. They shot out of her grey matter, causing the liquid in the jar to sizzle.

A movement caught my eye and I glanced up at the giant view-screen, which displayed an image of a fresh commotion outside Brainwaves. A sleek military helicopter hovered, the downdraught from its rotor blades blowing mopeds over as it slowly descended. The suspension on the undercarriage bowed as it took the full weight of touchdown. Star Squad Seven had arrived.

"Now, unscrew my jar," Lor-Ayn ordered. "For the transfer to work, it must be open."

I gripped the lid and immediately let out a yell. It was hot to the touch. Ignoring the increasingly uncomfortable sensation, I grasped it again and began to turn. Nothing. It was like the most stubborn pickle jar in the universe.

"Bang it on the table," suggested Lara.

"You will do no such thing!" snapped Lor-Ayn.

"In emergency, break glass?" suggested Sarah.

"You wouldn't dare!" said Lor-Ayn, but I could tell that she was wary of her former mind-slave.

"Come on, Luke," urged Zack. "Gotta get it open."

"Give it to me," ordered Miss Dunham, snatching the jar. But even with all her muscles and a lot of grunting she couldn't prise it off. The world was going to end

because we couldn't open a jar.

The phone burst into life. It was the colonel again. "Our Tracking and Imaging radar station reports zero contacts. If we can't find that missile platform, we can't destroy it. Any sign of Star Lad?"

"We're working on it," I replied, bracing the jar between my knees and applying both hands.

"Oh, this is so undignified," complained Lor-Ayn.

Just when I thought it was never going to budge, the lid moved exactly one millimetre and then all resistance fell away. It whirled off, dropping to the floor where it spun like a coin before settling on one side. Heads we win. Tails we lose.

Lightning leapt from the open neck of the jar. One jagged fork lodged itself in Zack's empty head and the lifeless body began to shake and moan. The Star Lad cape stretched taut, while the sigil on his chest blazed like Christmas lights (which was appropriate since I'd partially constructed it out of one). A second fork of lightning flew into my skull and I cried out. It was the worst headache I'd ever experienced, but it was worth it, because now Zack and I were joined to Zack's body through Lor-Ayn's lightning connector.

The mind-transfer was about to begin.

In just a few seconds Star Lad would be back in action.

"Do it!" yelled Zack.

There was a boom of thunder to accompany the lightning. The shockwave threw me backwards into Serge and Lara's arms. For a few seconds I felt dizzy. I shook it off and searched my mind for any sign of my brother. No complaints. No criticisms. And that lingering desire to revise for exams had vanished.

"She did it!" I said. "Zack's gone."

"Luke?"

It was Zack's voice...

"Where am I?"

...but not from Zack's body.

With mounting dread Lara, Serge and I lowered our heads level with Lor-Ayn's jar. The brain sat suspended in the gloopy liquid as before. The speaker crackled with Zack's panicking voice.

"What has she done to me?!"

Lor-Ayn had tricked us. Again.

My brother was a brain-in-a-jar.

23
JAR LAD

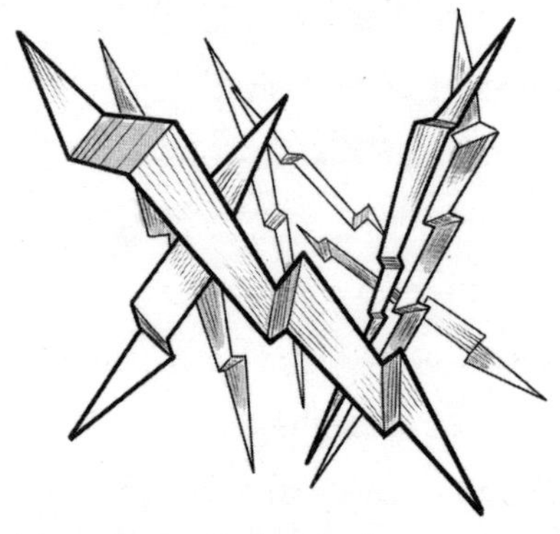

"Vile. *Re*-volting. I don't know how you can bear to be stuck inside all of this ... *flesh*."

Slowly, I turned to the source of the voice. There stood what at first glance appeared to be Star Lad; cape across his back, mask over his eyes. The newest occupant of my brother's body stretched out her arms and wiggled her fingers.

"So many moving parts." Lor-Ayn gave a shudder. "*Eurgh*."

Lor-Ayn had sent Zack's mind into her body, while inserting her own mind into Star Lad's.

"You ... you ... you're me..." stuttered Zack. It had

been hard enough for him to accept our body swap, so this latest switcheroo had him totally freaked out. He hadn't so much lost his mind, as found it in the worst place imaginable.

"And what's this thing beating under here?" She laid a hand on her chest. "You have a pump? Like a washing machine. Unbelievable."

While the rest of us struggled to come to terms with this latest reversal, Miss Dunham took action. In class, she'd always taught that the best defence is offence. Now she put her teaching into practice. With a yell she rushed at Lor-Ayn.

In response, Lor-Ayn sent a lazy glance in the direction of the approaching gym teacher. A force field rose up to block her path. It was mostly invisible, but where dust particles floated into the telekinetic shield they created sparks of blue light, like flies hitting a bug-zapper. Unable or unwilling to stop, Miss Dunham smacked against the field and bounced backwards through the air, hitting the floor with a thud.

If there had been any question in Lor-Ayn's mind about the success of the mind-transfer, then this demonstration answered it: she had control of Star Lad's powers.

"Impressive," she said, admiring her new abilities.

She wriggled her shoulders, trying to get comfortable. "Worth wearing this unpleasant body suit for." A triumphant grin spread across her face. It was Zack's skin, Zack's facial muscles, but the grin was all Lor-Ayn's. "My sister *will* be surprised."

So that was her plan. "You're going to take revenge on your sister using Star Lad's powers."

"Not Star Lad's any more," she gloated. "Mine. And once I've dealt with Mee-Grayn, I shall return to my world aboard *my* flagship and mete out *severe* punishment to every other Cerebran that exiled me."

She had successfully pulled the foil over our eyes. And while she flew away, the rest of us would be incinerated by the missile strike. In desperation, I tried to reach out to her…? Whatever the brain equivalent of "humanity" is called.

"Earth may have been your prison," I began. "But it was something else too. You made it your … holiday home. So for all the visitors to Great Minds who ever gave you a good review, for all of them who came back year after year, I'm begging you: stop the Muclear missiles." Perhaps I was hoping to appeal to some spark of kindness buried deep inside her. Perhaps I simply couldn't accept the unfairness of the situation, that two siblings falling out a long time ago could lead to the destruction of our planet. Either way, my words were a waste of precious breath.

Lor-Ayn threw back her head and attempted a mocking laugh, but though she was already accomplished with Zack's superpowers, she hadn't quite got the hang of his tongue. It flopped around in her mouth and the laugh dissolved into a lot of gagging. Eventually, she dislodged the tongue and recovered her composure.

"Now, if you will excuse me, I have to destroy my sister." She wobbled past us on equally unsteady legs, making for the lift.

Once she reached the surface it would be a moment's work for her to take to the skies. That would be the last we'd see of her. And we were powerless to prevent her.

"Stop!" The shout boomed from the Bluetooth speaker.

Lor-Ayn came to an immediate halt, frozen in place.

"You got *my* powers," said Zack-in-the-jar. "But guess what?"

Maybe we weren't quite as powerless as I'd thought.

"What?" said Serge, who was clearly struggling to keep up.

Lara rolled her eyes.

"No, I am serious," said Serge. "This is turning out to

be quite tricky to follow. It is like a game of ping-pong, but instead of a small plastic ball, the players are using minds."

Lara lowered her voice. "OK, so here's the situation," she began. "Zack is in the brain-in-the-jar, right? And Lor-Ayn is in Zack's body."

"*Oui*. I got that."

"That means Lor-Ayn now has all of Star Lad's powers, and Zack has…?" She paused to let Serge fill in the rest. Which turned out to be a mistake.

"Conflicted feelings?" he suggested with the air of a quiz show contestant who suspects he doesn't have the right answer.

Lor-Ayn was too busy to wait for Serge to get up to speed. "You fool," she snarled at Zack. "If I could have accomplished my goal while remaining in my own beautiful brain, do you think I would now be in your ridiculous body?" She pinched an armful of skin. "When I probed you for the first time I discovered something remarkable. Star Lad's powers are even greater than my own. There is nothing that you-as-me can do to stop me-as-you."

To give Serge his due, that was quite confusing.

With that, Lor-Ayn shrugged off the effects of the mind-control as easily as brushing a piece of fluff from a superhero cape and swaggered to the lift. It would've been more effective if the doors were already open when she got there, but first she had to spritz herself with perfume and then wait while the lift descended from the surface. She stabbed the call button a few times, presumably to hurry it up, but that never works.

"I-as-you may not be able to stop you-as-me," said Zack. "But I can do *this*."

Tiny sunbursts lit up inside the jar. Unlike Serge, I understood right away what was happening. Zack was attempting to trigger another mind-swap. My brilliant brother! If he could wangle his way back into his body then our problems were solved. But it was a big, brain-busting "if".

Just as before, the sunbursts gave way to lightning flashes of increasing intensity. He was doing it! When I'd occupied Zack's body I struggled to connect with any of his powers, but he seemed to have got the hang of Lor-Ayn's right away.

"I've got this, I've got this," he repeated. "I've…" There was a deathly pause. "…not got this."

A series of jagged lightning bolts blasted out of the jar and whizzed across the room, shooting off in random directions. It was like Thor having a tantrum. I threw myself to the floor and crawled under the nearest

computer station, covering my head with my hands. As I huddled there, hoping not to be hit by a stray bolt, I heard several violent bangs and crashes, followed by yelling and then silence. Gingerly, I lifted my head.

The bridge was a smouldering mess. Small fires had erupted across most of the control panels, patches of the deck were charred where lightning had struck, the giant view-screen was cracked and hanging at an unnatural angle. Automatic sprinklers kicked in, dousing the flames and creating a veil of smoke. Through the pall I could make out the others. They seemed to be in one piece, which came as a relief.

I crept out from my hiding place and glanced towards the lift. Lor-Ayn had gone.

Miss Dunham's stopwatch lay on the floor, presumably swept out of her hands by the blast. We had ten minutes before the world was blown to pieces.

Sarah crouched on the floor with her jacket over her head. Miss Dunham staggered out of the smoke, holding a corner of her tracksuit to her mouth. She lowered it, coughing. "Is everyone OK?"

"I'm fine, I think," said Lara cautiously.

She and Serge trailed behind the gym teacher, still wreathed in smoke. Through the grey cloud that covered them, I could make out their two figures shambling towards me.

"*Oui,* me also," said Serge, wheezing. "Hmm, I was sure that I brought my inhaler." He clapped his hands to his pockets, trying to feel for the elusive item. "Wait. These are not my trousers." His searching hands reached around to his back pockets. He peered over his shoulder. "And that is definitely not my *derrière*."

He and Lara emerged from the smoke at the same time. And stopped. They turned to face one another. The question of whether Zack's misfired lightning bolts had caused any damage beyond wrecking the command bridge had an answer.

"We have been ping-ponged," Serge muttered.

"Please tell me this isn't happening," said Lara.

But it was. My friends had swapped bodies.

There was a frustrated tut from Zack-in-the-jar. "Really thought I had it."

"I'm a boy," said Lara from Serge's mouth.

"I am a girl," said Serge from Lara's.

Which was kind of stating the obvious, but I guessed they were experiencing some sort of post-body-swap trauma. However, solving their gender-switch would have to wait.

"Lara, Serge, I need you to stay focused. You may have swapped bodies but you're still members of S.C.A.R.F.

The mission comes first."

Each of them nodded in shocked silence.

I lowered my voice to a whisper. "Anyway, it could be worse. You could've ended up like Zack."

"I heard that."

"Sorry. But your plan *was* a good one," I said. "You just need to try again, but this time hit the target."

"It may have escaped your notice," said Zack, "but our target isn't here any more."

"Then what are we waiting for?" said Miss Dunham, sprinting for the lift. "If we run our personal best we've a chance of catching up with her." She pushed the call button. The light remained dark and there was no sound of lift machinery. "I think Lor-Ayn has sabotaged it."

We tried the emergency exit, through which we'd gained access the very first time we'd attempted to infiltrate Brainwaves. Contrary to every health and safety requirement, it was sealed shut and the door wouldn't budge. We were trapped.

Though hanging off its mountings, the view-screen was still operational. On it we could only watch as Lor-Ayn as Star Lad made her way along Brainwaves' corridors. She was no more than a few minutes ahead of us, but right now even that small margin was a gulf.

"Can you attempt another mind-swap?" I asked.

"Let me try," said Zack. He fell silent for several seconds. "No good. This is all pretty new to me, but I think I need a clear sight of her."

"Last minute of the game and we're six points down," said Miss Dunham. "We need options."

My attention was taken by activity on the view-screen. Star Squad Seven cleared the last remaining children out of the water park and pushed everyone back to what they thought was a safe distance. Unfortunately, if we didn't come up with a plan right now the only safe distance would be Mars.

"Once Lor-Ayn accesses Star Lad's flying power," said Serge, "nothing on earth will be able to keep up with her."

"Nothing on earth," I mumbled, an idea forming. "Serge, you're a genius! There might be a way for us to catch her, but first we have to slow her down. Lara, your phone please."

Lara nudged Serge. "He means you."

"Ah, *oui*." Serge fumbled for the handset.

"Other pocket," said Lara helpfully.

He located it and passed the phone to me. There was one way to put the brakes on Lor-Ayn but no one was going to like it. "Colonel Crowe, how much firepower did Star Squad Seven bring with them?"

"Two unmanned drones in the air," he replied. "One fire-team on the ground."

"Listen to me. Star Lad has been taken over by an alien entity. When they see him they must treat him as hostile." I swallowed hard. "You have to neutralise Star Lad."

24
STAR SQUAD vs STAR LAD

"Negative," came back the response from Colonel Crowe. "You may be Star Lad's little brother but you have no authorisation to give such a command."

"Please, you have to try," I insisted.

"I may be the one out of my mind," raged Zack, "but you're crazy! Star Squad can't stop Star Lad. He is – *I am* – too powerful."

"I know that. I just need them to slow him down."

The liquid in Zack's jar streamed with bubbles. Maybe they were thought bubbles, because a moment later Zack said, "Colonel Crowe, it's me, Star Lad."

The colonel began to speak, but Zack cut him off.

"My little brother is right. You have to take down Star– me. Right now."

The main view-screen displayed the immediate consequences of Zack's words. The soldiers of Star Squad's sole fire-team positioned themselves either side of the entrance to Brainwaves. They crouched down, drew their weapons and waited for Evil Star Lad to emerge. If they could delay Lor-Ayn, then that would give me time to kick-start my last-ditch plan into action.

I turned to Sarah. "You said you were the pilot. So can you fly this thing?"

"Fly what thing?" said Zack, and then understanding hit him like a wooden plank to the back of the head. "Oh no. You can't be serious."

I'd never been more serious. "Once Lor-Ayn leaves the ground it's the only way to get you close enough. When we're in range, you can attempt another mind-swap."

The liquid in Zack's jar gurgled. "In case you'd forgotten, the last time Lor-Ayn and I were *in the same room*, I missed. The likelihood of me being able to pull off a successful mind-swap on the edge of space is—"

"All we've got," I reminded him.

"Target approaching." Colonel Crowe's voice burst

from the phone. He was patched into the soldiers' communications.

"I have eyes on Star Lad," said the leader. "Weapons free."

We glanced up at the screen and held our breath. The soldiers only saw Star Lad, but we knew that we were looking at Lor-Ayn. Nevertheless, it felt unnatural, watching Star Squad prepare to engage with Star Lad. In the end, there wasn't time for misgivings. Lor-Ayn swept past the soldiers before they could get a shot off, sending them sprawling with her telekinetic power. They tumbled to the ground like dolls thrown by an angry infant.

I snatched up the phone. "Colonel, you've got to give us more time."

"On it," he replied.

Sarah crossed to the crew station at the front section of the bridge, which I presumed must contain the flight controls. Her fingers moved expertly over a switch-heavy panel. She looked up with a worried expression.

"The screen, lights and air-conditioning are running off the mains," she said. "But that's the only power in the system right now."

It was more than fifty kilometres from the ground to the upper stratosphere. We weren't going anywhere on

mains power, not without a very long extension cord.

"Uh, Luke," said Lara. "Aren't you forgetting what the ship runs on?"

How could I forget? Lor-Ayn had planned to propel the Brainwaves craft through space using power drained from children's brains. I *had* taken that into account.

"Lor-Ayn needed enough fuel to escape Earth's gravity and transport her across vast interstellar distances. The amount of energy required for that sort of journey is literally mind-boggling. But if we don't plan on leaving the stratosphere, then all we need is a fraction."

"Just a few brains then?" suggested Miss Dunham.

Serge took a step forward. "I shall make the ultimate sacrifice," he said. "Use my brain." He raised a fist. "For planet Earth!"

"Yeah, nice," said Lara. "But remember that's actually *my* brain you're offering."

"Ah, *desolé*," said Serge.

"I don't need anyone's brain," I said, picking up Zack-in-the-jar. "Except yours."

With my brother objecting loudly as usual, I carried him to the crew station at the centre of the deck. I had identified it as the command chair, though it didn't look much like a regular chair. I decided it was where Captain Kirk would sit, if he were a brain-in-a-jar.

"Lor-Ayn is a powerful psionic being," I said. "She might not be a pool full of children, but I'm betting there's enough juice in this brain of hers to get the ship off the ground." I slid Zack into a circular groove and turned him like a key. The jar locked in place and lights fluttered on the command console.

"Something's happening," announced Zack. "Whoa! It's like a great, surge-y sort of whooshy… Oooh. Not entirely unpleasant. I feel a bit … light-headed."

The ship sprang to life as its vampire circuits sucked up Lor-Ayn's brainpower and distributed it to various systems throughout the vessel. A portion of the view-screen changed to a head-up-display and around it a collection of readouts. One of them was labelled "fuel status".

It stood at a big, fat zero.

"Come on," I urged under my breath. "Come on."

After what seemed like an age, the reading clicked up to "1%".

At the same time, on the other half of the screen, the helicopter rose into the air in a cloud of dust and mopeds. It climbed ten metres off the ground and settled into a hover. From there the pilot skilfully directed the downdraught from the rotor-blades against the approaching figure of Evil Star Lad. For a moment,

the force of the artificial gale did its job. He flailed like a mime walking against the wind.

"Power at five per cent," Sarah called out.

That didn't sound like nearly enough. "What's the minimum we need to get this thing in the air?"

"Fifteen per cent," she replied. "To be on the safe side."

On the screen, Lor-Ayn steadied herself, planting her feet firmly on the ground. Star Lad's cape streamed out behind her. And then with a casual flick of one finger she despatched the helicopter just as easily as she had the soldiers. The engine stuttered and the aircraft lurched through the air before flopping to Earth. It skidded across the ground, gouging a deep groove, and came to rest, rotor-blades buckled, but thankfully its fuselage intact.

"Colonel Crowe? Are they OK?"

"A few bruises but they're in one piece."

The power reading ticked up to "9%".

Evil Star Lad leapt into the air.

"Sorry, S.C.A.R.F. leader," said the colonel. "We couldn't stop him on the ground. I am tasking my UAVs to intercept. You should be able to see the plot on your screen."

Sarah hit a control and a sort of moving map overlaid

the main screen. It showed two small green dots closing on a third, red dot.

"Star Lad is in red," explained the colonel. "The two pursuers are our latest multirole Annihilator drones. Enough firepower and artificial intelligence between them to bring down a dozen squadrons of fighter jets and beat a roomful of chess grand masters, at the same time."

The Annihilators were fast and agile. They jinked left and right, changing direction at supersonic speeds with a suddenness that would overwhelm an ordinary pilot. They buzzed Evil Star Lad, initially doing a pretty good job of holding him up and buying us precious seconds. Star Squad's drones were good, but Evil Star Lad was better. I could see this dogfight ending only one way.

It was crunch time. "Colonel, I need the airspace over Great Minds cleared."

"Acknowledged, S.C.A.R.F. leader. To what altitude?"

I gulped. "All the way up."

The crew stations were designed for human occupants. While Sarah took the helm, the rest of us filled the remaining spots. As I took my place I noticed on the deck in front of my station was a pulsing circle of light. I stepped into it and felt my feet cling to the deck. The

glowing circle was some kind of high-tech seatbelt.

"Power at twelve per cent," Sarah called out.

I nodded. "It's now or never."

Lara shot me a glance. "She said fifteen per cent. To be on the safe side."

The countdown stood at four and a half minutes. "We're way on the wrong side of safe." We had to lift off right away, whatever the consequences. "Helm, report in."

Sarah surveyed her control panel one last time. "All systems nominal."

It was time.

I looked around at my friends, at Sarah and Miss Dunham, at my brother-in-a-jar. The only thing the crew of Brainwaves had in common with the legendary crew of the starship *Enterprise* was that we were all that stood between planet Earth and total destruction. It would have to be enough.

"So let me get this straight," said Zack. "In an attempt to catch up with the rogue mind occupying my body, you plan to fly an untested flying saucer piloted by a formerly brainwashed leisure centre host, and while we're zooming after Evil Star Lad at Mach 3 Point Nuts, you expect me to do that lightning jar trick again and swap minds with her in mid-air, then take out those invisible alien missiles?"

He'd understood perfectly.

I clenched my fist. "Launch!"

25
WHAT GOES UP

For a second nothing happened, and then I felt the tiniest of vibrations, a mouse-sized skitter that ran through the deck. That was instantly followed from deep within the bowels of Brainwaves by a rumble like a supernova clearing its throat to get the attention of a gamma-ray burst at the Annual General Meeting of Cosmic Explosions. The vibration built, joggling the view-screen and threatening to dislodge it from its already precarious position. The shaking became so violent that it reached through my skin and played my bones like a xylophone.

"Main engines online," shouted Sarah over the rising

clamour.

The alien propulsion system kicked in and as it did it made sense of the peculiar concentric ring design of Brainwaves. The outer ring began to spin in one direction, while the inner ring whizzed the opposite way. It was some sort of gyroscopic drive. I had a feeling all that spinning wouldn't be doing much good for the sandwiches in the Cortex Café.

I felt the deck tilt, and with one more complaining grumble Brainwaves rose into the air. The dangling view-screen showed us clearing the treetops. They swayed, bending back with the hurricane force of our passing.

"We're up," mouthed Serge in amazement.

Generally speaking, water parks are not meant to fly. So I could only imagine the surprise on the faces of the resort guests on the ground as they watched us climb into the cloud-streaked Thursday-afternoon sky. As Sarah adjusted our angle, tilting us to what felt like a vertical position, I was sure I could hear water from the swimming pools above sloshing about.

"Altitude one thousand metres," said Sarah. "Speed four hundred knots."

Those figures were good, but they stood in stark contrast to our fuel status. We'd set off with twelve

per cent and were already down to nine. Lift-off had consumed a hefty chunk of our reserves.

I studied the radar. It didn't do that sweep-thing you see radars do in films. This was alien technology, after all. It also didn't ping like a sonar in a submarine. Disconcertingly, it made the same tone that accompanied the park's PA system.

BING-BONG!

As Sarah focused on piloting the craft, Lara took over the role of calling out the numbers.

"Target at five thousand metres. And climbing."

Evil Star Lad was far above us, and getting away.

The Annihilator drones tried to keep him busy, but I could see from the radar that one of them was already down. As I watched the remaining drone cut across his path, it too vanished from the screen.

"Star Lad's taken out both Annihilators," said Colonel Crowe. "It's up to you now. Good hunting."

External cameras positioned on Brainwaves' outer surface fed visuals of our progress to the main screen. The water park bounced and shimmied as it shot into a layer of clouds, atmospheric dampers straining to smooth out our high-speed ascent. A second later we burst from the clouds into a clear blue sky. Sunlight danced off the hundreds of glass surfaces that formed the dome's shell.

It was very pretty. For a moment the beauty of the scene gave me an overwhelming sense of calm.

I checked in on my friends. Serge in Lara's body was coping with the buffeting ride, but Lara in Serge's body wasn't doing so well. His aversion to rollercoaster rides, which he'd kept hidden from her, was now uncomfortably obvious.

"Altitude eight thousand metre— *Eurgh*," she gagged.

From his jar, Zack let out a moan. Not the kind of moan he gave when I did something to annoy him. This was a sound of sheer agony. Stuck in Lor-Ayn's brain, the ship was sucking the life out of him too.

"Warning. Warning," an automated alert piped up. "Fuel status low."

On screen the number in question flashed red. It had dropped to seven per cent. We were burning up brain power faster than an ace student in a maths exam.

The water park climbed steadily, but at this pace we weren't going to catch Evil Star Lad in time. At the top edge of the radar display the target blip pulled away. Locked to it were speed and altitude data. The numbers raced up. Every metre took Lor-Ayn further from us and brought defeat closer.

"We're losing her," shouted Serge.

"We need more power," cried Miss Dunham.

"My mind. Can't. Take much more," Zack stuttered.

Lara called across from her crew station. "He's already giving everything."

But I had been in my brother's head and I knew that he had deeper reserves. "Come on, Zack, you've got it in you. All that maths revision you did instead of watching TV, all that extra physics homework you requested over the years. Your mind is more powerful than even you know."

"So. Much. Homework." He let out an anguished cry. On the main screen the fuel reading, which had sunk dramatically, now reversed its decline. It clicked up a single point.

That was all we needed. "Helm, give me warp speed!"

Sarah began to object. "Uh, we don't actually have warp sp—"

I cut her off. "Just go really fast – NOW!"

She pegged the controls, sliding them to their maximum setting, and the gyroscopic propulsion system went into overdrive. Brainwaves lurched upwards, my neck snapped back with the force of acceleration, the restraining circle on the deck held on to me by a big toe. The edges of the spinning rings glowed as they seared the air.

"Altitude twenty thousand metres," Lara called out.

On the radar the gap between us closed. Finally, we were gaining on our quarry.

"Altitude twenty-seven thousand metres."

We were on the edge of the stratosphere. Above us lay the darkness of space. I could see stars.

"Star Squad to S.C.A.R.F., come in. Over!" Amazingly, the voice came out of the mobile phone. Vodafone had better coverage than even they knew.

"S.C.A.R.F. receiving."

"Tracking stations have picked up a faint signal in low Earth orbit. It could be the alien missile platform. Sending coordinates to you now."

"Putting it up on the main view-screen," said Sarah. "Ten times magnification."

At first all I could see was the star-filled darkness and then I noticed a ripple in the void, like waves flowing over a stone. A moment later the stealth camouflage fell away, revealing the dark, angular form of the Cerebran missile platform.

"There is a peculiar reading on my screen," said Serge, tapping the console in front of him. "I have had absolutely zero real-world training but I have watched many science-fiction films and on that basis I propose that it is an energy spike from the alien weapon." He looked up. "The missiles are readying to fire."

The hand on Miss Dunham's stopwatch swept round for the last time. The countdown stood at forty-five seconds.

"S.C.A.R.F. to Star Squad. Can you take out the missiles?"

"Negative," came the reply. "Not in the time frame."

I turned to my brother. "Zack, if you don't deal with those missiles in the next forty seconds, then we're all dead." I gripped his lid and began to unscrew it. "You have to do the mind-swap, now."

"But how?" he protested. "I can't even see her."

"Listen to me, Zack," said Miss Dunham. "A good netball player doesn't have to look at her teammates or the opposition. She knows where they are. Where they're going to move. It's all about that first pass." It was like Obi-Wan Kenobi urging Luke to use the Force, if the Jedi master had been a gym teacher.

With one final turn, I wrenched the lid off.

Zack focused on the task. As before, sunbursts quickly appeared inside the jar and the gloopy liquid bubbled up.

I was just wishing that I felt as confident as Miss Dunham when Lor-Ayn's voice cut across my doubts. I could tell from the reactions of the others that they heard her too. She was using Star Lad's telepathic power to communicate with us.

"A worthy attempt, humans," she gloated. "But ultimately in vain. You're too late."

Her arrogance may have been her downfall. As she prattled on, I whispered to Zack. "Can you hear her?"

"Yes." He sounded weak. "She's in my head."

"Focus on the voice. You can use it to target her. Follow it back to the source."

"Like a thread in the labyrinth," Zack mumbled. I figured it was some kind of reference but I hadn't a clue to what. Probably some book. Why couldn't he stick to superheroes like a normal person?

"Soon I shall regain control of *my* flagship and my sister's jar will lie shattered at my feet," Lor-Ayn bragged. "Yes, now I can see the advantage of feet."

"Warning. Warning." It was the automated system again. "Fuel status critical."

Our burst of acceleration had all but exhausted our reserves. We were down to one per cent.

Inside Zack's jar, forks of lightning danced around the brain. He was building to the mind-swap. "OK, Lor-Ayn," he said. "I'm coming for you…"

Brainwaves slowed as it burned through the last drops of fuel, the water park's attitude adjusted, sinking on one side. Out of the view-screen I could see below us the

wide curve of the Earth.

"There she blows!" cried Zack.

Seriously, what was it with my brother and obscure references?

There was a flash as lightning speared from the open top of the jar. It shot straight up through the centre of the command bridge, a column of sizzling white fire piercing the roof. We followed it on the view-screen, watching it reach across the sky to find its target.

Hopefully.

The column of lightning lingered for a second and in that brief time I was sure I detected something wriggling along its length, like a fish glimpsed through deep water. Could it be Zack's mind leaving the brain?

And then it was gone, the crackle of energy replaced by an expectant hush. If the swap had been successful, Lor-Ayn should be back in her own brain. Quickly, I screwed down the lid to stop her reversing the mind-swap. I tapped the jar. Nothing. I tried again.

"Lor-Ayn? Hello?" It was possible that she was ignoring me, but I had a strong suspicion that was not the case. "Her brain is empty. She's not here." Something had gone wrong.

"Missile launch detected." When it came, the communication from Star Squad was remarkably calm.

"Multiple warheads inbound."

The Cerebrans had launched the salvo that would destroy Earth. The end of the world was shooting through the darkness of space at supersonic speeds.

"Warning. Warning. Fuel depleted."

We were running on fumes. Without engine power, the ship reached what was to be its highest altitude and began its inevitable descent.

The concentric rings of the gyroscopic drive ground to a halt. In the silence that followed there was a great creaking sound from the hull as Brainwaves tipped over. I felt my feet slip. Without power, the restraining mechanism couldn't keep us planted on the deck.

"Everyone, hold on!" I grabbed the corner of my console with both hands.

Great Minds had the worst attractions of any theme park I'd ever visited. But it was about to make up for that. A fifty-kilometre ride, straight down, ending with the biggest bang of the century as the planet blew up around us.

The ship angled nose-down and we plummeted through the thin air.

Lor-Ayn's jar slid from its mounting and crashed on to the deck. Sparks flew as circuits shorted out across the ship. The deck lights blew, plunging us into darkness

until an emergency backup kicked in, dousing us in an eerie red light. Why is emergency lighting always red? It's just unnerving. If they were like disco lights at least that would make everyone happy during a time of extreme stress.

I figured that the emergency generator must be operating on a battery – not enough to power the engines, just life-support systems and, by the looks of things, the view-screen too. One of the ship's remaining working cameras continued to feed images from outside, documenting our fall.

The Star Squad Tracking station chimed in with an update. "We are seeing a fast-moving object that appears to be on an intercept course with the missiles."

"Can you identity?" queried Colonel Crowe back at command HQ.

"Negative. Not one of our birds," replied the radar operator.

A bird was slang for a military aircraft.

"Can't be a civilian jet," he added. "Not at this altitude."

And in that moment, even as we fell towards the doomed Earth, I felt a flutter of hope.

It wasn't a bird. Or a plane.

It was Star Lad.

Zack had slotted himself back in his body. Game on! The view-screen displayed the same radar view that the Star Squad operators were watching. I followed the progress of his red blip as he caught up with the Cerebran barrage, represented by a series of yellow arrows, in the upper atmosphere.

"Missiles have altered direction," announced the operator excitedly. "They're heading away from Earth."

My brother was behind this latest turn of events, I could feel it.

"Luke, can you hear me?"

It was him, contacting me telepathically. "Loud and clear, Zack." Now that he'd dealt with the missiles, he was free to save us.

"Hold tight. I'm on my w—"

He was cut off before he could finish.

"Zack? You there? ZACK?!"

"Multiple missile detonations detected!" called the radar operator.

The view-screen whited out as the leading edge of the explosive shockwave rolled over us. The ship juddered.

The Cerebran warheads had exploded. The only consolation was that Zack had sent them far enough from Earth not to do any damage to the planet. But even as the danger to humanity shrank, his and our troubles

were looming. Powerless and flying blind, we sank lower in the atmosphere. Turbulence increased, icy winds pounded the water park, tearing off glass panels, howling in at the gaps. Without sophisticated flight systems to control our descent, we bounced all over the sky, at the whim of every gust.

Sarah fiddled with her controls and managed to get the view-screen back up. It was only partially functioning. The sensors were out of action so we didn't have radar. But I didn't need a fancy readout to tell me our altitude. The last remaining external camera delivered the bad news. We plunged through the cloud-base and I could see the ground below. Great Minds filled the view-screen. At this speed the impact would be catastrophic. We would wipe out everything and everyone for kilometres around. My mum and dad were down there.

"Can we fly this thing away from the resort?" I shouted to Sarah.

She shook her head.

I reckoned we had no more than five seconds before we crashed. I began to count down in my head.

"Five ... four ... three ... two..."

"One," said Zack.

It took me a moment to realise that Brainwaves had stopped moving. We were no more than twenty-five metres above the ground. Something caught my eye on the view-screen: a shape fluttering in the wind.

It was a cape.

Star Lad had swooped to the rescue, arresting our fall at the last second. Literally.

As it became clear we had dodged becoming the biggest (and saddest) pancake at Great Minds, the command bridge erupted with cries of relief. Lara-as-Serge hugged Serge-as-Lara. Miss Dunham was about to exchange shirts with Sarah/Saoirse when she remembered this wasn't the end of a football match, so they hugged too.

"Sorry about that." My brother's voice sounded in my head. "Got held up for a moment. All turned out OK in the end. Luke? You there? Speak to me."

My heart was pounding and I was too shocked to say anything at first. I pulled myself together to stutter out a reply.

"I..." I felt drained, shaky. I was definitely coming down with a cold. "I need a holiday."

But Zack had stopped listening almost immediately, distracted by something more important.

"*Eugh*, what's this stuck to my cape? Is that Haribo? *Luke!*"

26
MY ARCH-ENEMY

"Mmm, what a lovely, relaxing break," said Mum.

"Just what the doctor ordered," added Dad.

Only if the prescribing GP was Doctor Doom, I thought.

My parents glowed with well-being. Several days of enforced spa treatments had perked them right up. Given that on most normal days they were Mr and Mrs Bouncy Castle, this was bad news. I braced myself for an unbearably upbeat drive home.

The world had been saved and the holiday was over. We packed the car in preparation to leave Great Minds.

"Did you boys have a good time?" asked Mum.

"Hey, let's not shoot for the moon," said Dad, heaving the last suitcase into the boot. "Any answer without the phrase 'mind-numbing boredom' or 'I hate him' will do for me."

Zack and I exchanged looks.

"It was great," he said, and I mumbled my agreement.

Like the other adults at the resort, once the geranium brainwashing wore off, my mum and dad were none the wiser about the events of the last few days. Of course, loads of children had witnessed the remarkable flight of Brainwaves and I'm sure many of them attempted to inform their parents. But since Star Squad had taken care of all the phone video recordings there was no hard evidence. And would the mums and dads have believed them anyway? Doubtful. I think all the things that parents fill their heads with, like paying the bills on time and remembering to renew the car insurance, must block out the important stuff, like flying water parks.

Dad slammed the boot shut. It was time to leave. He paused, gazing out over the car park. A breeze ruffled his hair. "We need to treasure these times. It won't be long before Zack decides to go on holiday with his own friends."

Dad was prone to these outbursts about the future. He would come over all wistful, with an expression like

a sad Labrador, and say something to make Mum and him glum.

Hang on. "Do *I* still have to go on holiday with you?"

Dad sighed. "Yes, Luke."

"So if he's not coming, does that mean we can afford to go somewhere good? Like Disney World?"

"Oh, here's Serge," said Mum.

Serge-Who-Was-Still-Lara sauntered towards the car, having spent the last hour and half trying to say goodbye to Lara-Who-Continued-To-Be-Serge. Thankfully, I wouldn't have to put up with this body-swap nonsense for much longer. About an hour after we returned to Earth the plinth communicator had lit up with an incoming message. To my surprise, it wasn't Mee-Grayn or her sister. The holographic figure before us was the brain-in-the-dragon-jar who'd sat silently alongside Mee-Grayn during the first transmission.

"Greetings, Earthlings, I am Vascu-Litis. The *new* ruler of the Cerebrans."

It turned out that Mee-Grayn was just as unpopular as her sister, and while she'd been off trying to destroy the earth, there had been a palace coup back home. The Cerebran fleet had intercepted her flagship and now the sisters were aboard a prison transport. Vascu-Litis patched us into the ship's camera feed.

In a grey prison cell Mee-Grayn's familiar jar sat securely behind a force field.

"But where's Lor-Ayn?" I asked.

I hadn't realised that we'd also been patched into the ship's communication network, and she could hear me.

"Zuke Parker of Earth," Mee-Grayn said dismally. "I have played the game of jars. And lost."

"Why are you even talking to them?" It was Lor-Ayn. But I still couldn't see her. "You should've blown them up when you had the chance."

"Oh, do be quiet," Mee-Grayn silenced her sister. "And move over. You're touching *my* hemisphere."

I turned to Zack to find him sporting a small satisfied grin. I discovered that when he had performed his high-speed stratospheric mind-swap, he sent himself back into his brain – and deposited Lor-Ayn in her sister's. Obviously, he'd got the idea from our brief cohabitation.

"A fate worse than death," Zack mumbled.

The Cerebran sisters vanished into hyperspace, continuing to argue even as the prison ship was swallowed up by the vast darkness of the universe. They were welcome to each other.

"Personally, I would've sent them to the Phantom Zone." I saw the blank expression on Zack's face and

began to explain to him about the Kryptonian prison dimension. The blank expression remained and I gave up. He was a lost cause.

Vascu-Litis congratulated us on saving our planet and swore that the sisters wouldn't cause any more problems. "Now, is there anything I can do to atone for the crimes of my family?"

Lara immediately made a request for a mind-swap to return her and Serge to their own brains. It wasn't possible to carry it out there and then, but Vascu-Litis promised to send an emissary.

"I don't understand," Lara whispered to me. "Why is she promising to send a bit of a river?"

It took me a moment but I got there. "Um, not an *estuary*," I said. "An emissary is like an agent or a courier. I expect someone will show up with an antidote."

Lara wasn't happy about the delay; she was impatient to be herself again. However, Serge didn't complain. He had confessed to me that he was enjoying his residence.

"It is like another holiday," he had said. "On an exotic island, with a mysterious heart. And the fabrics..." He stroked a silky top of Lara's he had put on as soon as he could change. Then, for the only time, his ecstatic tone slipped. "Regrettably the food is entirely vegetarian."

Dad started the car. Serge-Who-Was-Lara slid in

beside Zack. I was about to follow when Sarah – now Saoirse – appeared. She had ditched her blazer and instead wore a smart grey business suit and carried a clipboard. She'd decided to stay on at Great Minds and make a go of running the resort. It turned out that being mind-controlled for years by an evil alien brain was an excellent grounding for a career in management. We said our goodbyes and she made us promise to return for another holiday, offering us a ten per cent reduction if we booked early. Which seemed a bit mean, given that Lor-Ayn had let us in free, even if it had been a ruse to steal my brother's superpowers.

"One thing I'd like to know," I asked her before getting in the car. "What did you do with Lor-Ayn's jar? Did you hide it in plain sight in a massive warehouse full of identical brains-in-jars, because that would be cool?"

"No, sorry, nothing that interesting," said Saoirse. "Let's just say this job generates a lot of paperwork." She winked at me.

I didn't get it.

"I don't get it," I said.

She sighed. "I'm using it as a paperweight."

There was the toot of a horn and a car bowled past us, heading for the exit. Josh hung out the back window, yelling at me and gesturing with something in his hand.

He was OK, no worse for being briefly mind-controlled. I started to wave back, heard the *pock* of a paintball gun firing, and looked down at my shirt, which now sported a fresh green splodge. I could hear Josh cackling until the car disappeared round the bend.

A few minutes – and a fresh shirt later – we too were on our way. Our car crested the hill with the giant billboard that overlooked the resort and Great Minds was behind us. I wouldn't miss the place. We began to descend the other side of the hill.

"You've got to be kidding," said Dad, glancing in the rear-view mirror. "It's that motorhome again."

I turned to look out of the back window. The radiator grille gleamed as the familiar white vehicle nudged close to our bumper. In the driver's seat I could see Miss Dunham. She was wearing a baseball cap, no doubt lined with extra-thick tinfoil. The human race would never know what it owed that gym teacher. She and I had been the last to leave the command bridge of Brainwaves. I'd asked about her plans – what was she going to do next? Would she return to her old life? She hadn't answered immediately. Instead, she'd stood in the centre of the deck with a distant gaze. "A storm is coming," she'd said.

"The forecast is for light winds," I told her.

Apparently she was being metaphorical. The Cerebran

threat may have gone, she went on, but the world wasn't safe. That was what she had learned. There were other perils out there, even stranger and more dangerous, and it was her job – no, her destiny – to be prepared for whatever came next.

"Well, come on then," said Dad, slowing down the car and steering it to the edge of the lane. "If you're going to pass, then get on with it."

As she drew level with us, I caught Miss Dunham's eye. For a moment I thought she smiled, but it was probably just a reflection from her tinfoil. She pulled out to overtake, passing us in a cloud of dust. And was gone.

A few days later found us back in the groove of regular life: Dad behind the counter at the comic shop, Mum at her desk in the insurance office. School had thawed out, and Zack was due to be debriefed by Star Squad that afternoon. I felt a twinge of envy that it was him and not me going to the Civic Centre this time. I hadn't exactly proved myself much of a superhero but I'd enjoyed the trappings. I'd miss that costume. The only blot on normality was that the Cerebran emissary had yet to show up, which left Serge and Lara in the same mixed-up pickle. The strain of being in each other's body was beginning to show. Lara had confided her unease to me

earlier that day.

"You know how a song sometimes gets stuck in your head and it just keeps going round and round and round?" I'd nodded and she went on. "Well, imagine that, but it's jazz. And not just any jazz, but French jazz."

Despite his initial enthusiasm, Serge too was experiencing anxiety. "I love sausages. Chipolatas, chorizo, *saucisson*. All kinds. But it is how they say," he lowered his voice, "you should never see how the sausage is made."

Thankfully, salvation was at hand. On the bus home after Zack's debriefing, he had received a telepathic message: the Cerebran ship was in orbit and the emissary's shuttle would be with us that afternoon.

"He or she is here," I said, peering curiously from the door of the tree house.

"About time," said Lara-Who-Was-Really-Fed-Up-As-Serge. She crossed her arms.

Serge-Who-Was-Lara grunted and turned his back. I had little sympathy for them. I'd told Serge, this is what happens when you start that whole dating thing.

There was a disturbance in the air as a vessel materialised level with the tree house. The Cerebran shuttle decloaked. It was a three-metre-tall jar, but made of an opaque material. There were no obvious hatches or windows, but as I watched, a seam appeared, describing a doorway. With a hydraulic hiss it lowered, clanking into place to bridge the gap between the ship and the tree house.

In the shuttle's doorway stood a tall figure wearing a black cloak, his face hidden by a cowl. In one thin hand he held a jar. Not a jar-with-a-brain; this one contained a single bolt of lightning. Without waiting for an invitation the emissary stepped silently across the bridge. We parted to let him enter the tree house. Something about the figure made me uneasy, but I couldn't put my finger on what it was.

Eager to begin the mind-swap, Lara-Who-Was-Serge tapped her foot impatiently to the rhythm of the music in her head. "About time. Now, can we please get on with this?"

The figure set down the jar and, gripping the edges of his hood, threw it back to reveal his face.

I gasped. It was a face that had once gazed at my brother and coveted his powers, a face that had stared down the Alien Overlord – a face I never expected to see again. But here he was, alive and … altered. What had once been human was now cyborg – a cybernetic organism. One eye was a large silver button with the word OK in its centre; his left cheek was a numbered keypad. And

as he reached for the jar I saw that one of his hands too was altered, replaced by a black oblong device inscribed with a word. I spelled it out. "S–O–N–Y." And then I understood.

He was half human, half TV remote control.

He clicked a button on the remote, activating a beam that held the jar steady, then clasped the lid with his other hand. "Shall we begin?" purred Christopher Talbot.

ACKNOWLEDGEMENTS

It takes a lot of mental energy to produce a book like this. Whether you're the brain-in-a-bar type or more brain-in-a-spa, I'd like to say thanks to all of you at Nosy Crow who lent your considerable grey matter. I am particularly grateful to the following people.

My editor, Kirsty "brain-in-a-star" Stansfield, Kate "brain-in-charge" Wilson, Catherine "campaign-in-a-jar" Stokes. And Adrian "meatballs-in-a-sauce" Soar.

My publicist, Clare "fame-in-a-jar" Hall-Craggs, Ola "brain-in-a-Eurostar" Gotkowska, copyeditor Hazel "eyestrain-in-a-jar" Cotton, and everyone at Bounce, the "brains-in-a-car".

Huge thanks as ever go to "crayons-in-a-jar" designer Nicola Theobald, and illustrators Rob Biddulph and Robin Boyden.

I'd also like to thank my agent, Stan. Interesting fact, did you know that agents only use between 10% and 15%

of their clients' brains?

Thank you to my two smart cookies: superhero-indifferent son, Luke, and dino-loving daughter, Lara.

And, finally, thanks to my wife Natasha, the missus of my amygdala, the one who makes my limbic system go loopy. No one can overstimulate my ventral tegmental area like you.